Copyright Page

© [2024], [Mohamed Elshenawy]

All rights reserved.

No part of this publication may be reproduced, distributed, or transmitted in any form or by any means, including photocopying, recording, or other electronic or mechanical methods, without the prior written permission of the publisher, except in the case of brief quotations embodied in critical reviews and certain other noncommercial uses permitted by copyright law.

First Published: [2024]

Publisher: [Mohamed Elshenawy "Self-Published"]

This is a work of fiction. Names, characters, places, and incidents are either products of the author's imagination or used fictitiously. Any resemblance to actual events, locales, or persons, living or dead, is entirely coincidental.

CH01456650

Beyond the Ice Wall
By Mohamed Elshenawy
"The Fourth Reich"

Table of Contents

Introduction to "Beyond the Ice Wall"

For generations, we have looked to the stars, believing the answers to our greatest mysteries lay in the vast expanse of the universe. But what if the truth has been much closer all along, hidden behind boundaries we were never meant to cross?

Dr. Ethan Cole, a brilliant scientist working for NASA, was drawn into a top-secret project—unlocking the power of a Stargate believed to transport humans to distant planets. What he didn't expect was for the gate to lead him to a hidden realm right here on Earth. Beyond the frozen ice wall, Cole discovers a reality that shatters everything he knows about our world.

Joined by investigative journalist Lena and a rebellious group of green-skinned inhabitants, Cole finds himself in a battle for survival against the Reptilians, powerful beings who control this hidden realm. As he uncovers the shocking truth about the Controllers—ancient forces manipulating humanity for centuries—Cole must decide how far he's willing to go to expose a truth that may be too dangerous to reveal.

Beyond the Ice Wall is an epic journey of discovery, mystery, and survival. It explores the boundaries between reality and conspiracy, blending science fiction with mind-bending revelations. The more you uncover, the more you question what's real—and what's not.

Prepare for an adventure where science, myth, and cosmic forces collide. This is not just a battle for survival; it's a battle for the truth.

About the Author: [Mohamed Elshenawy]

I am Mohamed Elshenawy, a passionate writer of science fiction, horror and fantasy, with a love for weaving intricate stories that blend the speculative with the mysterious. My works often challenge the boundaries of reality, exploring themes of conspiracy, hidden truths, and the vast unknowns of our universe.

Alongside writing, I bring a diverse background as a. Fluent in multiple languages, I draw inspiration from global cultures, myths, and science, creating stories that resonate with readers from all walks of life.

In *Beyond the Ice Wall*, I aim to take readers on an unforgettable journey that questions everything we think we know about our world—and the forces that control it.

"The Fourth Reich"

Chapter 1: Escape and Discovery

We tumbled out of the portal with an unsettling jolt, landing hard on the smooth, mirror-like surface beneath us. My lungs struggled to catch a breath as I scrambled to my feet, dragging Lena up alongside me. The disorienting journey through the portal left us both dizzy, our senses muddled, but the suffocating intensity of this place quickly snapped us back to reality.

The air here was thick, almost metallic, with a strange, unsettling taste that lingered in my mouth. It felt heavy, pressing down on us, as though the atmosphere itself wanted us to stay still. I scanned the area, my vision clearing enough to take in our surroundings. Everywhere I looked, the landscape mirrored our reflections, casting warped, distorted images back at us. The ground shimmered with an eerie iridescence, reflecting the strange silver sky above, where clouds twisted and swirled unnaturally fast, as if time was somehow off-kilter here.

And that's when I felt it—a heavy, ominous shadow sweeping over us, blocking out what little light there was. I looked up, my heart sinking as I saw the massive creature above, its wings stretching wide, casting an intimidating shadow across the landscape.

"Run!" I shouted, gripping Lena's hand as I pulled her forward. The dragon, with its metallic scales glinting like polished steel, circled above, its fiery gaze locked onto us. Its massive wings beat the air, creating gusts that rattled my bones and whipped Lena's hair around wildly.

We sprinted across the mirrored ground, our footsteps slipping on the surface that felt as if it would crack under our weight at any moment. The dragon let out a deafening roar that echoed across the silent expanse, a roar that carried a terrifying promise. Fire seethed at the edges of its maw, and with a mighty thrust of its wings, it dove toward us.

"Left!" I shouted, dragging Lena with me as we veered sharply. We dodged to the side just as a torrent of flame erupted from the dragon's mouth, scorching the ground we'd just abandoned. The heat radiated through the air, intense enough that I could feel it prickling the back of my neck.

Lena gasped for breath, her eyes wide with panic. "Ethan, we can't outrun it!"

I knew she was right. This creature was faster, stronger—utterly relentless. But then, out of the corner of my eye, I noticed something unusual. A faint light glowed in the distance, flickering like a beacon against the alien landscape. It was artificial, unmistakably so, and in this place, it was our only chance.

"There!" I pointed, my voice strained. "The light! Head toward it!"

Without a second thought, we bolted toward the light, our steps quickening with renewed desperation. The dragon circled overhead, watching, waiting, its massive form casting ominous shadows across the ground as it followed us.

We closed in on the source of the light, and as we drew closer, the shape of an enormous structure began to take form through the haze. My heart skipped a beat as the details came into focus—a massive compound, cold and imposing, with high walls and guard towers that seemed almost ancient. Barbed wire stretched along the top, and in the dim light, I could make out symbols on the walls. They were faint but unmistakable: the harsh angles of a swastika.

I exchanged a horrified look with Lena, whose face had gone pale. "No way," she whispered, her voice trembling. "That can't be real."

"It is," I murmured, barely able to comprehend it myself. "But this... it doesn't make sense."

We crept forward, keeping to the shadows cast by the compound walls. The dragon, its interest waning, let out a final roar before it veered away, flying off into the silvery sky. Relieved but on edge, we found ourselves caught between one nightmare and another.

We reached the edge of the compound, pressing ourselves against the cold metal of the wall, hidden in the deep shadows. I dared a glance over the edge, and what I saw made my blood run cold.

Soldiers, dressed in familiar, horrifying WWII-era uniforms, marched methodically along the compound's perimeter. Their coats bore swastika patches on the sleeves, and their faces were stern, disciplined, and hardened. I felt a chill as I realized these men looked out of place, but not because of their uniforms—it was as if they had been pulled straight from history and preserved in perfect form.

"Are we... in the past?" Lena asked, her voice barely above a whisper, her gaze fixated on the soldiers.

I shook my head, my mind racing. "No... I don't think so. This feels... different. It's almost as if we've stumbled into some kind of alternate realm. Somewhere that's... outside of time."

Lena swallowed, her eyes never leaving the soldiers as they passed in crisp formation. "This has to be some kind of... stronghold. A hidden place where they... escaped?"

"That might be it," I replied, adrenaline still pounding through my veins. "If what we're seeing is real, then we're looking at a world that shouldn't exist."

We remained hidden, watching as the guards patrolled the compound's perimeter. They moved with eerie precision, their faces blank, as if marching to a rhythm only they could sense. There was something unsettling about this place, as though it had been preserved from some darker chapter of history. I couldn't shake the feeling that this was another secret held tightly by the Controllers—perhaps a realm given over to people who should have been forgotten.

But what was this place? And why were its inhabitants so familiar, so hauntingly out of place?

"We have to get out of here," Lena whispered, her voice tight with unease. "This place feels... wrong, Ethan. Like a nightmare from a history book."

I nodded, glancing around for an escape route. The compound was enormous, fortified with high walls and barbed wire. The dragon had moved off into the distance, but with the soldiers here, we were still too exposed. There was no way out by force alone.

"We need to find a way to open another portal," Lena suggested, her eyes darting nervously as a new patrol of soldiers rounded a corner. "We can leave this place behind before they even know we were here."

"Agreed," I murmured, feeling a flicker of hope. "Let's keep low and quiet until we find a secure spot to use the Stargate device. With luck, we'll be gone before anyone realizes."

We edged along the compound's outer walls, keeping close to the cold metal as we moved. Just as I reached for the Stargate device, a sudden shout rang out, cutting through the still air.

"Halt!"

Lena and I froze, our eyes wide. Several soldiers in dark uniforms spotted us from across the compound and immediately began advancing. Panic flared in my chest, but there was no time to act, no time to run. We were cornered, surrounded by armed men who blocked every exit.

"Don't move!" one of the soldiers barked, his weapon trained on us. More soldiers joined him, their faces expressionless, their rifles trained steadily.

Lena shot me a desperate look, but I could only shake my head. There was no way out.

Within moments, the soldiers reached us, yanking our hands behind our backs and binding them tightly. They searched us, their movements quick and efficient. My heart sank as one of them found the Stargate device attached to my belt. The soldier examined it with a look of suspicion and curiosity before handing it over to an officer, who tucked it away without a second glance.

"Move," one of the guards ordered, prodding us forward with the butt of his rifle.

Lena's face was pale as we were marched through the compound, past rows of tents and barracks. The structures were adorned with flags bearing symbols that made my stomach twist—the dark red banners, the familiar black swastika. It was like stepping into a twisted version of the past, an unsettling mirage where remnants of history clung to life.

The soldiers led us to a dimly lit corridor beneath one of the larger buildings. The air here was thick, almost suffocating. The faint smell of dampness and rust mingled with the dust that clung to the stone walls. With each step, I felt as though we were descending further into the belly of some hidden beast, a place where shadows and secrets converged.

We stopped at the end of the corridor, facing a heavy metal door that loomed before us. One of the guards unlocked it, and with a creak that echoed down the hallway, the door swung open.

"Inside," the guard ordered, shoving us forward.

We stumbled into a small, windowless cell, its bare walls lined with rough stone, illuminated by a single, flickering light. A single metal bench was bolted to one wall. The guards unfastened our bindings and stepped back, their expressions as blank as ever. I tried to catch one of their eyes, hoping for some flicker of understanding or pity, but their gazes remained distant, unreadable.

"Wait here," the officer said, his voice as cold as the cell around us. "Someone will be along shortly to question you."

With that, the guards stepped out, the door slamming shut behind them. The lock clicked into place with an unsettling finality, sealing us in. Lena and I were alone, trapped in a cell in a world that seemed frozen in a dark history that neither of us understood.

Lena slumped onto the bench, burying her face in her hands. "They took everything," she muttered, her voice muffled. "The Stargate device, the frequency weapon... everything."

I leaned against the cold stone wall, my mind racing. Without the Stargate device, we were stuck here—wherever *here* was—at the mercy of a group that seemed to have stepped out of history itself.

I swallowed, pushing back a surge of panic. "We're in trouble, Lena. Big trouble. And we don't even know who these people are or what they plan to do with us."

She looked up, her eyes red-rimmed with fear but laced with determination. "Ethan, we have to find a way out of here. There has to be something we can do. We can't just sit here and wait to be... questioned."

I nodded, forcing myself to stay calm. "You're right. We'll get through this. Somehow. We just need to stay sharp and be ready for any opportunity that comes our way."

But as I scanned the small, suffocating cell, my heart sank. There were no windows, no vents—nothing that even remotely resembled an escape route. With our equipment confiscated, we were as helpless as prisoners from a century ago, trapped in a nightmare we barely understood.

The minutes passed in silence, each one stretching longer than the last. The cold seeped through my clothes, biting at my skin as we waited, the steady drip of water somewhere in the darkness our only companion. I could feel the weight of the place pressing down on us, the walls seeming to close in with each passing moment.

And then, without warning, the door swung open.

Lena and I looked up, startled, as two guards stepped into the cell. Their faces were as blank as ever, their movements precise and controlled. They motioned for us to stand, gesturing for us to leave the cell.

"Time for questioning," one of them announced, his voice flat, devoid of any trace of humanity.

Lena cast me a nervous glance, but I gave her a reassuring nod, hoping to convey a confidence I didn't feel. This was our only chance to gain any insight into where we were, who these people were, and what exactly was going on. We had to play along, at least for now.

The guards led us through another dimly lit corridor. The walls seemed to close in around us, the air thick with an unspoken tension. My mind raced as we moved deeper into the compound, my heart pounding with a mixture of fear and curiosity.

Who were these people? Why had they taken us prisoner? And what could they possibly want to know?

The reality of our situation was sinking in fast, but there was still so much we didn't understand. These soldiers bore the symbols of a dark past, but what did they hope to achieve here, in this strange, hidden world? And how much of this place did the Controllers truly know?

One thing was clear: we were in a world where history's shadows still loomed large, a place where things that should have faded into memory had somehow found new life. And with our technology in their hands, these people now held the key to our only escape.

Lena and I exchanged a glance, a silent promise to face whatever lay ahead together. No matter what they had planned for us, we weren't going down without a fight.

Chapter 2: The Interrogation

The guards escorted us down a cold, dimly lit corridor, our footsteps echoing through the stone passage. The silence was oppressive, broken only by the occasional shuffle of the guards' boots. I could feel Lena's tension beside me; her shoulders were stiff, her gaze hard as she walked, but a flicker of fear haunted her eyes. I shared that fear, the deep, unsettling sensation that we'd stepped into a world built on shadows and deception.

Finally, we arrived at a heavy metal door. The guards unlocked it and nudged us inside. I took a breath, noting the smell of metal and stale air as we entered the room. The starkness of the space only heightened the dread coiling in my stomach.

The room was dominated by a cold, metallic table bolted to the floor, with two chairs positioned opposite each other. The fluorescent lights buzzed faintly, casting a sterile, almost surgical glow across the surface. It was an unsettling blend of antiquated design—straight out of some mid-century bunker—and advanced technology, with sleek, unrecognizable panels blinking in low, eerie rhythms along the walls.

The guards instructed us to sit, then left without another word, the door slamming shut behind them with a resounding thud. A heavy silence fell over the room, and I felt the weight of it pressing down on us.

Lena whispered beside me, her voice barely audible. "What is this place, Ethan?"

I shook my head, unable to answer. The longer we stayed here, the more disoriented I felt. Nothing about this situation made sense—our captors seemed caught in a strange mixture of past and present, as though they belonged to another era but wielded power beyond our understanding.

A few minutes passed, stretching into an uncomfortable silence. The tension hung heavy in the air, and every tick of the clock felt like a countdown to something unknown and dangerous.

Then, the door opened again.

A man entered, dressed in military attire that was strikingly familiar—dark, with sharp angles, meticulously pressed. His face was set in a stern expression, and his posture held an unsettling rigidity. Every movement he made was precise, mechanical, almost as if his body operated by gears rather than muscles. He stood before us, scrutinizing us with an intense gaze.

"Welcome, foreigners," he said, his voice laced with a thick German accent. His gaze swept over us, landing on the logos stitched on our clothing. "Or should I say... trespassers?"

I exchanged a quick, uneasy glance with Lena. The man's formal, almost theatrical way of speaking seemed to come from another era, and yet his words were chillingly direct.

"You are out of bounds," he continued, his gaze narrowing. "This area is strictly controlled, and individuals such as yourselves are of particular interest to... the mission."

I swallowed, my mind racing. The mission. Whatever it was, it was clear we'd been seen as more than intruders. There was something they needed from us.

"Your names," he demanded, his tone as flat and unfeeling as the room around us.

"Dr. Ethan Cole," I replied, struggling to keep my voice steady. "And this is Lena."

He inclined his head slightly, as if filing the information away. Then he crossed his arms and looked at us with cold calculation. "You will answer our questions, Dr. Cole, Ms. Lena. Any attempt to deceive us will be... severely discouraged."

The implied threat sent a chill down my spine, but I maintained eye contact, hoping to show no fear. Lena stiffened beside me, but her gaze remained steady.

The interrogator paused, studying us with an unreadable expression. "Explain to me," he began, his tone low and controlled, "how you came to be here in Area 50. And," he added, his eyes glinting, "the means by which you traveled."

I hesitated, unsure of how much to reveal. The Stargate device had been our escape, our lifeline. I wasn't about to give it away so easily, even if they had confiscated it.

"We... stumbled across a doorway," I said cautiously. "It was by accident. We didn't mean to intrude."

The interrogator raised an eyebrow, clearly unimpressed. "Do not waste my time with feigned ignorance. The device you carried is no ordinary 'doorway.' It has significant properties—properties of interest to us. Explain its workings."

I shot Lena a glance, hoping she understood the silent message: play it down, deflect. We couldn't afford to let them know the full extent of the Stargate's power.

"It's... experimental," I said, carefully choosing my words. "A prototype for testing spatial coordinates. We weren't even sure it would work."

The interrogator leaned forward, studying me intently. His gaze was sharp, probing, and I had the unnerving feeling that he could see right through me. "And yet, you appear here—uninvited and out of place. Tell me, Dr. Cole, do you truly expect us to believe that this was all... happenstance?"

I said nothing, hoping silence would serve as a shield. But it was clear he wasn't finished.

He folded his arms, his gaze shifting between Lena and me. "Your attire," he noted, eyeing the NASA insignia on our suits. "Area 51, correct? You and your associates believe yourselves to be... guardians of some higher knowledge, do you not?"

Lena stiffened, and I felt a jolt of surprise. How did he know about Area 51? And what exactly did he know?

The interrogator smiled, a cold, humorless expression. "You are not the first from Area 51 to trespass. The Controllers have seen to that. But your technology—the device—is unusual. A means of travel they have yet to share with us."

His words hung in the air, charged with a strange intensity. I glanced at Lena, who looked as baffled as I felt. The device—the Stargate—it was clear they knew of its significance, even if they lacked the means to control it themselves. And for reasons still unclear, they seemed to envy our connection to the Controllers.

"Allow me to enlighten you," he continued, his voice dropping to a conspiratorial whisper. "You are currently in Area 50. This is our realm. Our territory. One which we acquired with our own strength and determination."

I tried to keep my face impassive, though my mind was reeling. Area 50. It sounded like something out of a science fiction story, yet here we were, surrounded by people who operated under a different set of rules—perhaps even a different version of history.

He straightened, his expression hardening. "It was not our choice to abandon your so-called Area 51. We did not wish to leave the public eye. But certain... agreements were made with the Controllers. Agreements that ensured our survival and the establishment of the Fourth Realm."

The words sent a chill through me. This was not just a hidden compound, not just a base for renegades. This was an entire society—a regime allowed to thrive in secrecy, its past horrors preserved under the watchful eye of these Controllers.

"You and your people operate under the illusion of control," he continued, his voice dripping with disdain. "But here, in Area 50, we answer to no one. We have built a new order, a Fourth Reich—a realm of true power. The Controllers may observe, they may advise, but they do not command us."

Lena's hand tightened on the table, and I could feel the tension radiating from her. The scope of what he was describing was too vast, too horrifying to fully comprehend. The Controllers had made deals with the Allies to allow Area 51 to operate in secrecy, yet here we were, face-to-face with a new and terrible reality—a hidden empire created in parallel to ours, forged in darkness.

The interrogator leaned forward, his eyes narrowing. "So I suggest, Dr. Cole, Ms. Lena, that you cooperate. We have no interest in playing games, and your assistance could be... beneficial. But," he added, his tone darkening, "should you withhold information, we will be forced to use other methods. Perhaps methods you have read about."

The threat hung heavily in the air, and I could feel Lena tense beside me. I forced myself to remain calm, even as my mind raced with questions and fears. This was no idle threat; this man had made it clear that they possessed the power to act without restraint, and the Controllers' shadowy influence only heightened their sense of invincibility.

The interrogator studied us both for a long moment, as if weighing our reactions. Then, with a curt nod, he rose from his chair.

"Consider my words carefully," he said, his voice cold and final. "You are now part of history's preservation, whether you choose to cooperate or not. The Reich has endured long enough to know how to obtain the answers it requires."

Without another word, he turned and left the room, leaving us in silence. The door closed with a hollow thud, and I heard the lock click into place, sealing us in.

For a moment, neither of us moved. The weight of his words, the implications of everything he'd revealed, settled heavily in the air.

Lena leaned closer, her voice barely a whisper. "Ethan, this is... it's beyond anything I could have imagined. An entire society—hidden from history. This Fourth Reich..."

"I know," I replied, my voice strained. "The Controllers... they've let this happen. They've allowed these people to build a realm outside of time, hidden from everyone. And now, they want us to help them."

Lena's eyes were dark with determination. "We can't stay here, Ethan. Whatever it takes, we have to find a way out."

I nodded, feeling the weight of our predicament. The Fourth Reich held us captive, but we weren't about to give them what they wanted. No matter what, we had to find a way to escape.

Chapter 3: The Fourth Reich Unveiled

The guards entered our cell with a synchronized precision that was almost mechanical, their faces blank and unyielding. They gestured for us to follow without a word, their movements so uniform that they seemed more like extensions of the cold, concrete walls than men. I exchanged a wary glance with Lena, who looked as tense as I felt, and we braced ourselves, falling in line behind them.

The corridors were dim, the silence broken only by a faint hum from unseen machinery that reverberated through the walls. At the end of the hallway, we were led through a pair of reinforced doors. As they swung open, the atmosphere shifted entirely.

We stepped into a vast, high-ceilinged laboratory, where rows of machines and monitors lined every wall, their screens flashing intricate streams of data. The air was sharp with the scents of chemicals and sterilizing agents. Scientists in immaculate white uniforms moved with quiet purpose, each absorbed in their work. There was a disquieting order to everything—no mess, no clutter, every piece of equipment positioned with clinical precision.

One figure stood out among the lab coats. A woman with a sharp gaze and poised stance was positioned beside a large monitor displaying a map that appeared to span not only this realm but several others. She turned as we approached, her eyes intelligent and piercing, assessing us with a cold, hungry curiosity. Her face betrayed an undercurrent of excitement, almost as if she were restraining herself. When she spoke, her voice was smooth, deliberate, and accented with a precise German edge.

"Dr. Cole," she acknowledged, dipping her head slightly. "I am Dr. Klara Weiss, chief scientist here. I've heard a great deal about you—and about your... unique device." Her English was flawless but carried an unsettling weight, each word meticulously chosen.

I inclined my head cautiously, meeting her stare. Her gaze lingered on me with an intensity that bordered on possession, as if I were a prized specimen she longed to dissect.

"Your Stargate device," she continued, her tone reverent, "is remarkable. We have theorized such concepts, but the Controllers... well, they have withheld access until now."

A tension settled between us as I weighed my response. "It's... certainly unique," I replied neutrally, refusing to reveal too much.

Dr. Weiss smiled—a slight, pleased curve of her lips—then gestured to the machines around us. "This lab is the heart of our research, on the edge of Area 50, situated just beyond the main city and near the frontier. Beyond this realm, there are countless others." She pointed to the large map displayed on one of the monitors, showing a complex network of sectors divided by barriers, both natural and artificial. A massive ice wall was prominently marked, clearly indicating the border of Area 50. Beyond that lay realms known only by numbers.

"These divisions are intentional," Dr. Weiss explained, a hint of reverence in her voice. "The Controllers have crafted each realm, preserving specific... attributes within. Each area serves a unique purpose, ensuring that the world maintains its delicate order."

Beside me, Lena shifted uncomfortably. "So the Controllers keep everyone confined, sorted by area?" she asked.

Dr. Weiss's lips curved faintly. "Precisely, Ms. Lena. This place is built on discipline, on order. Here, we are liberated from the chaos of your world. We pursue a new vision, free from the... misunderstandings of the past."

As she led us through the laboratory, she pointed out various projects in controlled scientific fields. Her pride was unmistakable, and the entire setup seemed meticulously designed to ensure absolute control over every variable.

Finally, we exited through a door at the far end of the lab, emerging onto a wide avenue where the city stretched out before us.

It was a city unlike any I'd seen—each building a model of streamlined uniformity, all bearing the same sleek, faceless architecture. Yet what struck me most were the symbols adorning every surface, carved into walls, emblazoned on flags, stamped onto pavements: the swastika. It was everywhere, woven into the very fabric of this place.

As we walked, Dr. Weiss continued to speak as if reciting a creed. This city is but one of countless others in the vast network of the Fourth Reich. Here, every leader, scientist, and soldier is devoted to a vision of a perfected society—untainted by the distractions of lesser ideologies and unified in purpose.

Screens mounted on nearly every building displayed a loop of propaganda videos: families of various races, including green- and blue-skinned individuals, working side by side in staged harmony. The footage was unsettlingly idealized, showing faces of disciplined contentment. I felt a chill realizing this was not mere fiction—here, order was absolute, enforced with unwavering pride.

Lena leaned close, her voice barely above a whisper. "Is that—?"

"Yes," I muttered back. The streets weren't populated solely by people of European descent but included others, categorized and dressed in distinct uniforms. Each group moved in perfect unison, another cog in a meticulously ordered machine.

Even children marched in formation, clad in identical uniforms, their eyes devoid of wonder, fixed straight ahead. No bustling crowds, no laughter—just a society functioning with the eerie precision of clockwork.

As we continued, we passed towering statues of Adolf Hitler, each meticulously maintained, his cold visage looming over the streets. The citizens passed the statues with solemn nods, as if paying homage to the figurehead of this shadow society.

A dark, identical fleet of cars lined the roads, each one bearing the swastika and moving in exact intervals. Everything here—people, machines, even the air—seemed to conform to an unyielding vision of absolute order.

The general we'd met earlier reappeared, striding toward us with a purpose. "Dr. Cole," he greeted me, his eyes unreadable, "welcome to the Fourth Reich. This society was built on strength, on unity. Here, the vision endures, evolved and perfected."

He gestured to the screens above, which continued to display scenes of workers, soldiers, citizens moving with rehearsed precision. On one screen, a figure stood before a crowd, delivering an inaudible but impassioned speech.

"This," the general declared, "is what humanity can achieve when freed from the distractions of disorder. Here, we build with purpose, transcending the petty squabbles of your world."

I felt Lena's hand tighten around mine, her face barely concealing her disgust as she scanned the screens, as though seeking some flaw, some crack in this perfectly rendered illusion.

The general turned back to me, his expression hardening. "We understand you hold knowledge, Dr. Cole. Technology that could allow us to breach these boundaries without the Controllers' constraints. Your device is of... particular interest."

I met his gaze, keeping my voice even. "And if we refuse?"

His eyes narrowed, his voice dropping to a frigid tone. "I'd advise against such defiance. Cooperation will be... well-rewarded. But refusal? Discouraged." His smile was thin, his eyes sharp. "The Reich has many methods, Dr. Cole. I'm sure you'd find our persuasion techniques quite... familiar."

A chill traced up my spine, but I held his gaze. "What would you have us do?"

He gestured toward the city. "First, understand what we have built here—the strength, the order. Then, we'll talk again. Perhaps you'll appreciate the role you might play in our vision."

With a curt command, he directed the guards to return us to our quarters. As we were led away, the weight of what we had seen settled heavily within me. This was no mere relic of a dark past—it was an oppressive machine of control, an entire world crafted from the darkest visions of history.

Lena and I shared a look, a silent promise. We had to escape. We had to expose this twisted society to the world.

Chapter 4: Encounter with the Impossible

The cell's steel walls felt suffocating, their cold, unforgiving surfaces pressing in on us like a constant reminder of our entrapment. Lena and I sat on the narrow bench, leaning close and speaking in low, urgent whispers. The flickering light overhead cast faint, jittery shadows across the room, amplifying the tension between us.

"We can't just sit here, Ethan," Lena said, her voice firm but controlled. "We need to get that Stargate device back, and we need to find a way out."

I nodded, but my mind was already turning over the obstacles we'd have to face. "It's not going to be easy. They're watching us like hawks. And that general..." I paused, a flicker of frustration flaring within me. "He'll never let it go willingly. They want that device as much as we do—maybe even more."

Lena's eyes searched mine, as if hoping for some trace of a plan. "So what's our move?" she pressed, her brow furrowed. "Play along? Pretend to cooperate until they let their guard down?"

"Possibly." I kept my tone cautious, not wanting to raise her hopes too much. "We need to find out where they're keeping it first. If we can locate it, maybe we can grab it when they least expect it." I glanced at her, feeling a pulse of resolve. "But we can't rush this. If they even suspect us, the whole plan's finished."

Lena exhaled sharply, pressing her lips into a thin line. "But how long can we wait? They have guards posted everywhere. They're just waiting for us to make a wrong move." She crossed her arms, frustration darkening her face. "It's like we're rats in a cage."

"Then we'll have to make an opportunity," I said, the weight of the plan settling over me like lead. "If we can distract them or make them think we're cooperating, maybe they'll relax their watch, even if just for a moment."

A heavy silence filled the room as we let the gravity of our situation sink in. Lena's gaze drifted to the floor, her shoulders sagging slightly. I knew she was struggling with everything we'd seen here—the chilling streets, the cold perfection of the place, the eerie discipline of its people.

"Ethan," she murmured, shaking her head slowly, "this city... it's like they've taken everything awful from that era and preserved it, turned it into some kind of... machine." She glanced at me, her eyes dark with disbelief. "I keep thinking none of this can be real."

"It shouldn't be," I said, a shiver running down my spine. "It's like a nightmare brought to life. And they're just... living it. Like it's all they know."

Lena shuddered, her voice tinged with sorrow and disgust. "These people move like cogs in some vast machine. Everything is so regimented, so devoid of humanity." She looked away, her jaw clenched tightly. "Even the kids, Ethan. They don't even act like kids."

The memory of those blank, expressionless faces—children marching in perfect rows, eyes fixed forward without a hint of curiosity—flashed in my mind. "They've stripped away everything that makes people human," I murmured. "And the Controllers... they've let it thrive, kept it hidden away, twisted."

The silence returned, but a new resolve burned within me. "We can't just escape, Lena. If we get out, we need to bring proof of this place with us. People have to know."

Lena's gaze sharpened, meeting mine with a spark of determination. "Then we're going to need more than an escape plan—we need evidence."

I nodded slowly. "Once we secure the Stargate device, we'll find a way to expose everything."

The silence was broken by the sound of metal scraping against metal—the unmistakable click of a key turning in the lock. Our heads snapped up as the door swung open, revealing the general flanked by two guards, their faces as stoic as the steel walls around us.

"Dr. Cole, Ms. Lena," the general intoned, his voice as calm and unyielding as ever, "you are summoned."

Lena's brow furrowed, a spark of defiance in her eyes. "Summoned by whom?"

The general's mouth curved into a thin, humorless smile. "The Führer has requested your presence."

A cold shock sliced through me, and I felt my pulse quicken. I exchanged a glance with Lena, her face mirroring my disbelief.

"The Führer?" I echoed, barely able to get the words out. "You mean... Hitler?"

The general's gaze remained steady, almost reverent. "Yes. Our Führer has survived. Thanks to the advancements of our scientists, he remains with us, guiding our Reich, even in his advanced age. He is eager to meet those who hold technology that could secure our future."

My mind reeled. Hitler would be more than a century old by now, a relic of the past—yet here we were, being told that he still lived. I turned to Lena, her face pale with disbelief.

"That can't be," she whispered. "It's impossible."

The general's eyes glinted with pride. "Our scientists, under Dr. Weiss, have pioneered advanced preservation techniques. The Führer's life has been prolonged to continue leading us." He gave a slight nod. "Consider yourselves honored. Very few are granted an audience."

My stomach twisted, nausea creeping over me as I tried to process the impossible. This was something out of a nightmare, but the general's conviction left no room for doubt.

The guards led us through winding corridors, Lena's face tense with disbelief, her gaze flicking between the guards and me. The general strode ahead, each step heavy with quiet reverence, his demeanor brimming with a solemn pride. The thought weighed heavily on my mind—meeting Hitler, alive, should be impossible.

"Ethan," Lena whispered, barely audible, "this can't be real. Hitler? Here?"

I shook my head, just as bewildered. "Feels like a nightmare," I murmured. Part of me hoped this was some twisted game, an elaborate bluff. But the general's unwavering reverence had a conviction that sent a chill down my spine.

We arrived at a pair of guarded doors, the soldiers on either side as motionless as statues. The general stepped forward, entering a code. With a low hum, the doors unlocked, opening to reveal a dim, sterile room.

A thick antiseptic smell hit us immediately, laced with the hum of machines—a complex network of whirring devices surrounded a bed in the center, cables weaving around it like dark veins. And lying within this web of machinery was a face that seemed plucked straight from history, a figure of pale, ghostly skin stretched thin over frail bones. It was Hitler.

I froze, my mind struggling to process the sight before me. He appeared impossibly aged, his body almost skeletal, more connected to the machines than free from them. But his eyes—focused, cold, and calculating—pierced through the air, sharp with a disquieting intensity.

The general stepped forward, his voice filled with reverence. "Führer, these are the ones responsible for the technology we discussed."

Hitler's eyes shifted toward us, his gaze dark and assessing. When he spoke, his voice was a raspy whisper, hollow yet commanding, filled with an unsettling authority.

"So," he murmured, "the Americans bring technology of consequence."

A chill crawled up my spine as his gaze lingered on us. Lena's hand brushed mine, grounding me. Hitler's expression shifted as he observed us, his eyes narrowing, and he gestured weakly to the general, who took a respectful step back.

"What do you want with the device?" I managed, my voice tense and barely controlled.

A thin, almost spectral smile flickered across Hitler's face. "I imagine you were told many things about me, about the war," he said, his words laced with a strange relish. "But I am here to tell you that everything you know... is a lie."

Lena drew in a sharp breath, her disbelief mirroring mine. "What are you saying?"

"The war," he began, his voice growing in fervor, "the Allies—they didn't fight for freedom. They made a pact with the Controllers. They agreed to a system where power would never lie with the people."

Silence fell, his words seeming to echo, bouncing off the cold, clinical walls.

"The Controllers created them, molded them. The Allies struck their deal, securing a world forever ruled by forces you'd never even imagine. The Third Reich," he said, his voice gaining an almost haunting resonance, "was the last stand—an attempt to keep control where it belonged: with humanity, not with them."

Lena's voice was laced with skepticism. "Are you really expecting us to believe that?"

Hitler's eyes flashed, his faint smile vanishing. "You've seen what lies beyond the ice walls. You've seen what they tried to bury." His tone grew venomous. "The Allies helped create the Controllers' vision, painting their own version of history, which you've accepted blindly."

The enormity of his claims struck me like ice water. The idea that the world we knew had been crafted and controlled, that our history was shaped by hidden forces—it defied belief. Yet here, facing this hidden empire, it felt like truth's shadow was lurking just beyond the light.

"I saw through them," Hitler continued, his voice filled with unsettling conviction. "I sought to control, yes—but to keep the world free from the Controllers' dominion. They craved subjugation; I fought for sovereignty. But that, of course, is not the history you learned."

I wanted to protest, to challenge him, but words escaped me. Every instinct rejected his narrative, yet his tone, this place, seemed to tangle reason with an inescapable sense of something darkly possible.

"After the war, after we were forced to retreat," he continued, his voice tight with bitterness, "we came here, granted this place as part of a truce. An agreement that we would remain, silently building the Fourth Reich, separated from your Earth as long as we didn't interfere."

"What's changed?" Lena asked, her voice steady despite the weight of his words.

"The Controllers grow bold," he replied. "Your NASA—their NASA—is the tool they use to enforce their lies. Everything you know about Earth, space, the universe beyond—designed to keep you contained, obedient. You were taught the Earth is a globe so you'd never question its edges, told of galaxies to keep your gaze turned upward, away from the borders of your reality."

The room seemed to shrink around us, his words thickening the air with an oppressive weight. His claims stirred thoughts I didn't want to entertain, ideas I'd never allowed myself to consider.

"We don't need your device," he said, his eyes narrowing. "You may keep it. But we need the technology it uses—to open a gate large enough for our return, to re-enter Earth and reclaim what is ours. This Fourth Reich, this realm—it was never meant as the end. Only a beginning."

He paused, his eyes locking onto mine with unsettling intensity. "Join us. Use your device to help us open that gateway. Together, we can break the Controllers' hold on Earth, tear down the lies."

The room fell silent, his words hanging heavily between us. My pulse thundered in my ears as I glanced at Lena, her face drained of color, her expression caught between disbelief and horror.

"You don't need to decide now," he said, his tone softening, almost persuasive. "Think it over. You've seen what we've created, seen the city. Imagine the world we could build without these chains. This isn't a prison—it's a waiting room. A place we were given to hold us back until the moment was right."

"We're not here to help you conquer Earth," I said, my voice trembling but resolute. "We came here by accident, and all we want is to go home."

His thin smile returned, an eerie satisfaction glinting in his eyes. "I understand your reluctance. But remember, the world you return to was crafted by those who have deceived you your entire lives. The Controllers hold the reins, and you are merely their pawns. Choose to return, and you embrace their illusion."

The general stepped forward, his voice steady and unyielding. "Consider your decision carefully. The Führer grants you freedom to choose, but this offer is not given lightly."

Lena took a step back, her voice barely a whisper. "We need time."

"Time is yours," Hitler murmured, his tone chilling. "But remember, the choice is not merely between sides. It is a choice between truth and illusion, freedom and submission."

The general gestured, and the guards stepped forward to escort us out. As I cast one last look at the figure on the bed, surrounded by the machinery sustaining his frail form, I felt a dark weight settle over me. This man—once a name we thought buried by history—now claimed to hold the keys to a twisted, hidden order.

The doors closed behind us, sealing us back into the winding maze of corridors, but his words lingered, heavy and cold, gnawing at the edges of my mind.

Chapter 5 The Point of No Return

The guards escorted us back to our quarters in silence, the heavy door clanging shut behind us. Lena and I exchanged a look, our expressions mirroring the same stunned disbelief. The room felt colder, heavier, thick with the weight of what we'd just learned from Hitler himself.

"Do you... believe him?" Lena whispered, as if saying it out loud might solidify the horror.

I shook my head, still trying to process the encounter. "I don't know. But something in what he said..." I trailed off, leaning against the metal wall, running a hand over my face. "The Controllers, the lies about Earth, the Stargate—there's a twisted logic to it, like pieces of a puzzle forced together. But it doesn't make it any less terrifying." I glanced at her, urgency flaring in my eyes. "We have to get the Stargate device and leave."

Lena nodded, her expression hardening. "And expose all of this. If there's even a fraction of truth in what he said, the world has to know."

Silence filled the room, interrupted only by the distant hum of machinery. The enormity of our situation settled on us like lead, and a plan began to form. "If we can secure the device and open the Stargate, we might just get out of here. Get back to Earth. Warn everyone."

Footsteps suddenly approached from outside, and Lena and I exchanged tense glances as the door swung open, revealing Dr. Weiss flanked by two guards. Her expression was intense, her eyes steely and unyielding.

"Dr. Cole," she said, her voice taut, "the Führer has issued new orders. You're to join me in the lab now. We have urgent work to complete."

My pulse quickened. This could be our only chance—or a trap.

Dr. Weiss led us through the facility's winding corridors at a brisk pace. At last, we arrived at the lab, and there it was—the Stargate device, positioned on a raised platform at the center of the room. Its metallic surface gleamed beneath the harsh lights, and a spark of hope surged in me as I met Lena's gaze.

"Dr. Cole," Dr. Weiss commanded, her tone impatient, "demonstrate your device. Show us how it functions."

My fingers brushed the device's cold surface, every part of me on edge. "This technology is complex," I replied, buying time. "It requires exact calibrations to stabilize the portal. One mistake, and it could destabilize entirely."

Dr. Weiss's expression tightened. "Then make no mistakes," she snapped, stepping back, her eyes never leaving me.

Keeping my movements slow, I began adjusting the dials and settings on the device, whispering to Lena, "Get ready. This might be our only chance."

The lights flickered as the device powered up, casting an eerie blue glow that bathed the room. The edges of the portal began to shimmer, and I felt my pulse racing. We were close.

"Careful..." I murmured, inching the dials forward, but just as I made the final adjustment, the lab door swung open. The general strode in with two additional guards, his face stern and impassive.

"The Führer has arrived," he announced with authority. "He wishes to observe the demonstration himself."

The guards parted, and Hitler entered the room, leaning on a cane. His frail frame seemed at odds with the dark, commanding intensity in his gaze. His eyes moved between Lena and me, lingering on the Stargate device with a look of fervent satisfaction.

"Dr. Cole," he said, his voice low but resolute, "you have done well to deliver this to us. Now, you will complete your purpose."

I felt my throat tighten. "And what purpose would that be?" I asked, forcing my voice to remain steady.

Hitler's lips curled into a faint smile. "To bring us home. The Controllers think they've confined us here, that we would simply wait, powerless. But with this technology..." He gestured to the Stargate, his eyes alight with dark triumph. "With this, we can open the gate wide enough for an army."

Lena's body tensed beside me as realization dawned. "You're planning to invade Earth?"

His gaze shifted to her, unchanging, unfeeling. "Not invade. Reclaim. We will restore the Reich, and with it, the world will finally be liberated from the Controllers' deception."

"You can't do this," I said, barely able to keep the tremor from my voice. "If you tear through these realms, the consequences—"

"The consequences," he interrupted, his voice icier than before, "are precisely what we need. Humanity has been shackled, forced to believe in fabrications about planets, about the nature of space—all constructed by those who are unworthy of such power. We will bring true freedom, Dr. Cole. And it starts here."

He turned to the general, a fierce glint in his eye. "Prepare the troops. It is time we fulfill the mission I began long ago."

The general nodded, his face set with grim determination. "At once, Führer."

I watched in horror as Hitler moved closer to the Stargate device, his withered hands tracing its edges with almost reverent touch. "Soon, Dr. Cole," he murmured, "this device will open the doorway to Earth. And the Fourth Reich will complete what it began."

He turned to the guards, his eyes blazing with purpose. "Begin preparations for the invasion."

The guards saluted, and the magnitude of his words crashed down on me like a weight of iron. An invasion. They were planning to seize Earth by force, with no regard for the lives they'd destroy, all under the guise of "freedom."

Lena grabbed my hand, her grip iron-tight. Fear mirrored in her eyes as she whispered, "We can't let this happen, Ethan. We have to do something."

Hitler's gaze returned to us, his expression a warning and a promise all in one. "Take them to secure quarters," he ordered, his tone chilling. "We will need them alive until the gate opens. After that, they are expendable."

The guards closed in, gripping our arms as they led us toward the door. Just before we crossed the threshold, I cast one last glance at Hitler. His expression was filled with twisted satisfaction, an unshakable certainty that his twisted vision was within reach.

The doors shut behind us, and as the guards marched us down the corridor, Lena and I shared a look, silent but resolute. We had to find a way to stop them. We had to act—and we had to act fast.

Part 2 Earth Invasion
Chapter 6: Preparing for War

The room they had locked us in was nothing short of a prison, albeit one wrapped in a deceptive cloak of modernity. Stark metallic walls surrounded us, reflecting the harsh, clinical light from a single, recessed fixture in the ceiling. There were no windows, save for a small glass slit high up in the door, barely wide enough to allow us a glimpse of the cold, unforgiving reality outside. Yet that narrow window was enough to show us what was happening beyond these walls—just enough to spark a chilling understanding of the situation we were up against.

I paced the room, my mind spinning with the implications of Hitler's words, the implications of everything we had seen. I stopped mid-step, staring out of that small window. Outside, soldiers moved in synchronized patterns, their expressions vacant but their movements disturbingly focused. They were preparing, moving with an urgency that bespoke a singular purpose. And that purpose, as Hitler had made clear, was Earth.

Lena sat on the narrow metal bench, her face drawn and tense. I could see her mind working, running through possible escape plans as quickly as they formed. But she, like me, was at a loss. Everything we thought we knew had been shattered, every belief challenged, every assumption thrown into question.

"Ethan," she whispered, her voice barely audible over the silence. "We can't just sit here. We have to do something."

I stopped pacing, feeling the same sense of desperation gnawing at me. "I know," I said, struggling to keep my voice calm. "But we're in their territory. They've got our Stargate device, they've got the technology, and..." I glanced toward the slit window again, where soldiers with futuristic weaponry marched in organized lines. "And they've got an army."

Lena let out a shaky breath. "I keep thinking... what if he's right? What if everything we've been told about Earth, about the universe... it's all lies? What if they're really coming to take Earth back from the Controllers?"

I wanted to dismiss the thought, to reassure her that Hitler's words were just the delusions of a madman. But a part of me wasn't so sure. The Controllers, the hidden technology, the ice walls surrounding the different areas of this strange world... It all fit, somehow, in a twisted, horrifying way.

Still, I shook my head. "It doesn't matter what he believes," I said firmly. "He's still planning an invasion. If he thinks he's liberating Earth, that makes him even more dangerous. Fanatics are always the hardest to reason with."

We sat in silence for a moment, each lost in our own thoughts. I looked over at Lena, and her eyes met mine. "We have to escape," she said, her voice steady now. "We have to stop this."

I nodded, feeling a newfound resolve settle over me. "Agreed. But we need a plan—and some kind of ally on the inside."

As if on cue, we heard footsteps outside our door. I tensed, and Lena straightened up, both of us watching as the door swung open. A guard stepped in, his face mostly obscured by the shadow cast by his cap. But there was something different about him, something in the way he glanced around quickly before shutting the door behind him.

He stepped closer, lowering his voice. "Dr. Cole? Lena?"

We exchanged a confused glance. "Yes," I replied cautiously. "Who are you?"

The guard looked over his shoulder one last time, then leaned closer, whispering urgently. "My name is Lukas. I don't have much time, but I need you to know—I don't believe in this madness."

Lena's eyes widened. "You don't... believe in it?"

Lukas nodded, his face tense. "I joined the guard to survive, to protect my family. But what Hitler and the generals are planning..." He shook his head, his voice filled with a mix of disgust and fear. "It's going to bring unimaginable destruction. And it's wrong."

My mind raced. Could we trust him? Was this some kind of trick, a trap to see if we'd cooperate? But as I looked into his eyes, I saw something genuine—a glimmer of fear, yes, but also a determination that couldn't be faked.

"We're here against our will," I said cautiously. "We never intended to bring the Stargate device to them. In fact, we want to stop this invasion."

Lukas nodded. "I figured as much. I overheard some of the higher-ups talking. They know that you two have been trying to resist, trying to hold back information. But they've already modified the device. It's... it's ready."

A cold dread settled over me. "Ready? What do you mean?"

"The device," Lukas explained in a rushed whisper, "has been modified to create a one-way portal to Earth. It's stable enough to transport troops, vehicles, even their new drones. The plan is to initiate the portal within hours."

Lena and I exchanged horrified glances. This was happening far faster than we'd anticipated. If they launched this invasion, Earth wouldn't be prepared. The advanced weaponry, the cloaking technology... It would be chaos.

"Lukas," Lena whispered, urgency coloring her tone. "Is there any way to stop it? To disrupt the portal?"

He shook his head. "Not without alerting the entire compound. Security is at its highest level right now. But..." He hesitated, glancing around again as if someone might be listening.

"But what?" I pressed.

"There might be a way to sabotage the troops themselves," he said, his voice barely above a whisper. "The invasion will initially target specific locations—major global capitals, places with strategic importance. If you can warn the people there, even delay their response time, it might buy you some time to find another way to stop them."

"Warn Earth?" Lena murmured, her eyes narrowing in thought. "How? We don't have any means of communication."

"I can help with that," Lukas replied, pulling a small, outdated-looking radio device from his pocket. "It's old tech, but it's reliable and doesn't leave a digital footprint. You might be able to use it to send a signal—something subtle, something that won't immediately give you away."

I took the radio, feeling a surge of hope. "Thank you," I whispered. "But... why are you doing this? Why risk your life for us?"

Lukas's expression hardened. "Because I believe in freedom, true freedom—not this twisted version they're trying to sell. And if there's a chance to stop them... then I'm willing to take that risk."

With that, he moved to the door, pausing for just a moment. "Be careful," he warned. "The generals are watching you closely. Don't do anything rash until you're ready."

He slipped out of the room, leaving Lena and me alone once more. The silence that followed was thick with tension, but this time, it was laced with a glimmer of hope.

Lena turned to me, her eyes determined. "We have to use this radio. Even if it's a long shot, we have to try."

I nodded, already thinking of ways to encrypt a signal, to send out a message that would make sense to those on Earth but remain subtle enough not to alert our captors.

Over the next hour, I worked with the radio, adjusting the dials, testing frequencies. It was a clunky, outdated device, but Lukas had been right—it was reliable. Finally, I found a frequency that might work, one that would reach Earth's communication networks without drawing too much attention.

I crafted a short, coded message, something that would make sense to those who knew me but hopefully confuse anyone else.

"Attention. This is Dr. Ethan Cole. Critical threat approaching from unknown origins. Warn capitals. Prepare for an unprecedented attack. Trust no one."

I hesitated for a moment, my finger hovering over the transmit button. But then I pressed it, watching as the signal went out, hoping against hope that someone would pick it up, that someone would listen.

When it was done, I set the radio aside, feeling both relief and dread. We'd done what we could to warn Earth. Now, we needed a plan for ourselves.

Through the small window, we could see soldiers gathering, organizing in terrifying precision. They wore a mix of old and new—uniforms reminiscent of Nazi Germany but equipped with sleek, advanced technology. Their weapons looked like something out of a sci-fi nightmare, combining brute force with refined, almost elegant design. And they were ready, fully prepared to march through the portal and take Earth by storm.

"It's happening," Lena murmured, watching in horror. "They're actually doing it."

I clenched my fists, anger and helplessness welling up inside me. "We can't let this happen. We can't."

At that moment, Lukas returned, his face grim. "The signal went out," he whispered. "I intercepted the feedback. Someone on Earth picked it up. They're preparing as best they can."

A sliver of hope pierced the darkness. But Lukas's next words dampened it.

"The portal opens in one hour," he said quietly. "They're moving out. And once they're through... Earth won't stand a chance."

Lena grabbed my hand, her eyes blazing with determination. "We have to do something. Now."

I looked at Lukas, searching for any hint of a plan, any clue that he had a way out. But he only shook his head. "I've done all I can. But I believe in you both. If anyone can stop them, it's you."

With that, he gave us a nod and slipped out, leaving us to face the chilling reality of what was about to unfold.

And as I watched the soldiers prepare, I made a silent vow. I would find a way to stop this invasion. I didn't know how, I didn't know what it would take, but I would find a way.

Because the fate of Earth depended on it.

Chapter 7: Escaping Captivity

The silence of the cell was punctuated only by the hum of distant machinery and the muffled sounds of soldiers marching outside. Lena and I sat huddled in the corner, whispering in low tones, forming our escape plan. Every minute that ticked by was one step closer to Hitler's forces storming through the Stargate, and we couldn't let that happen.

"We need to move fast and be prepared for anything," I murmured, glancing at the makeshift tools we'd managed to gather, courtesy of Lukas. They were rudimentary—a screwdriver, a small blade, a roll of wire. They weren't much, but in the right hands, they could be enough.

Lena nodded, her expression set in determination. "First, we need to get past the guards at the door. Lukas said they're on a strict rotation, so we'll have only a small window."

I took a deep breath, feeling the weight of the plan settle over me. "We'll take them out quietly, no noise, no mess. After that, we head straight down the eastern corridor. Lukas said that route leads to a restricted area with minimal guards, mostly scientists. If we can find a computer terminal, we might be able to get intel on their plans and find an exit route."

She nodded, her eyes fierce and focused. "Let's do this."

The sound of footsteps echoed down the hallway, signaling the approach of the guards. Lena and I exchanged a look, silently moving into position on either side of the door. I held the screwdriver tightly in my hand, my pulse quickening as the footsteps grew louder, stopping just outside the door.

With a metallic click, the door swung open, and two guards stepped inside. They scanned the room briefly, not expecting any trouble.

That was their mistake.

Before they could react, Lena moved swiftly, striking one guard in the throat, cutting off his air with a silent choke. I lunged at the other, driving the screwdriver into his shoulder, using the element of surprise to unbalance him. He struggled, but with a quick, precise twist, I knocked him out cold. Lena's target went limp as she released her hold, and within seconds, both guards lay unconscious on the floor.

"We're clear," she whispered, her breathing steady but intense.

I nodded, my adrenaline spiking. "Let's move."

We slipped out of the cell, leaving the guards behind as we navigated the dimly lit corridors. The facility was vast, a maze of cold metal walls and clinical lighting, each corner more foreboding than the last. We moved quickly but cautiously, keeping to the shadows, ducking into doorways and alcoves whenever we heard voices or footsteps approaching.

As we moved deeper into the complex, the sounds of machinery grew louder, and we began to hear fragments of conversations between the scientists and soldiers we passed. They were talking about the invasion—about the "return to Earth" and the "reclaiming of the Reich." Each word fueled my resolve, reminding me of what was at stake.

We reached a small maintenance room and ducked inside, catching our breath. Lena glanced around, her eyes sharp as she took stock of the space. "We need to find a terminal soon," she whispered, glancing at the door. "They're already talking about the invasion as if it's guaranteed."

I nodded, feeling the pressure mounting. "There has to be a control room or data hub somewhere nearby. Lukas mentioned that the eastern section was where the scientists kept their equipment and schematics. Let's head that way."

Carefully, we cracked open the door and peered out, checking for any signs of movement. The corridor was clear, so we slipped out and continued our silent trek, hugging the walls and staying alert.

After a few tense minutes, we found what we were looking for—a small room off the main corridor, filled with computer terminals and buzzing with activity. It was empty, likely due to the staff being preoccupied with the invasion preparations.

Lena moved to one of the terminals, her fingers flying over the keyboard as she worked to bypass the security protocols. I stood guard by the door, my eyes scanning the corridor for any signs of approaching footsteps.

"Hurry," I whispered, feeling a knot of anxiety tighten in my stomach.

"Almost... there," she murmured, her face illuminated by the glow of the screen. After a few seconds, her eyes lit up in triumph. "Got it. I'm accessing their files."

As Lena navigated the system, I glanced over her shoulder, watching as lines of data flashed across the screen. She pulled up documents detailing the invasion plan—maps of Earth's major cities, lists of targeted locations, and diagrams of their advanced weaponry.

"They're planning to hit every major capital," she whispered, her voice filled with horror. "New York, London, Moscow... all at once. They're going to cripple Earth's defenses before anyone even knows what's happening."

I clenched my fists, anger boiling inside me. "We have to stop this. Download everything."

Lena nodded, quickly transferring the files onto a small flash drive she'd hidden in her jacket. Just as the progress bar neared completion, we heard footsteps approaching. My heart skipped a beat as I glanced at the door.

"Someone's coming," I whispered urgently.

Lena yanked the flash drive from the computer and shut down the terminal. We barely had time to duck behind a stack of crates in the corner as two soldiers entered the room, their voices carrying over the low hum of the computers.

"I heard the invasion's happening sooner than planned," one of them was saying. "The Führer himself gave the order."

"Good," the other replied, his tone cold. "Earth has been under the Controllers' thumb for far too long. It's time we take back what's ours."

Lena and I exchanged a horrified glance. Hitler was pushing the timeline forward. We didn't have as much time as we thought.

The soldiers lingered for a few more seconds, checking some equipment on the other side of the room. I held my breath, my heart pounding as we waited in tense silence, hoping they wouldn't spot us.

Finally, the soldiers finished their check and left the room, their footsteps fading down the corridor. I exhaled in relief, glancing at Lena. "That was too close."

She nodded, her expression grim. "We need to get out of here, now. I managed to download a map of the facility's layout, along with the invasion plans. This will help us navigate the way to the Stargate device."

"Good," I replied, feeling a renewed sense of urgency. "Let's move before anyone else shows up."

Following the map on the flash drive, we slipped through the facility, sticking to the quieter sections where we were less likely to be spotted. The hallways were dimly lit, and the faint hum of machinery filled the air, giving the entire place an eerie, lifeless quality. The corridors seemed to stretch on endlessly, each one identical to the last, creating a disorienting maze of cold metal and harsh lighting.

At one point, we ducked into a supply room to avoid a passing patrol. We pressed ourselves against the wall, holding our breath as the soldiers walked by, their heavy boots echoing in the confined space. I could feel Lena's pulse racing as she stood beside me, the tension palpable.

When the patrol passed, we continued on our way, our eyes sharp, ears straining for any sound that might indicate an approaching threat.

Eventually, we reached a door marked "Restricted Access." According to the map, this was where they stored the high-level equipment and information—the technology powering the Stargate and the weaponry they planned to use in the invasion. It was heavily guarded, but we didn't have a choice. We needed that information if we were going to have any hope of stopping this.

Using the tools Lukas had provided, I managed to bypass the lock, and we slipped inside. The room was filled with rows of servers, computer terminals, and large screens displaying complex data streams. At the center of the room was a holographic display of Earth, with several points marked in red—no doubt their intended targets.

Lena moved to one of the terminals, inserting the flash drive and downloading as much information as she could. I stood watch, my nerves on edge as I scanned the room, feeling the weight of our situation pressing down on me.

Suddenly, the door opened, and a scientist entered, his eyes widening in surprise as he saw us. Without hesitation, I lunged forward, knocking him out before he could raise the alarm. Lena shot me a quick look of gratitude, and we continued our work, downloading the information as quickly as possible.

Just as the download finished, an alarm blared, its shrill sound echoing through the facility. Our cover had been blown.

"Time to go," I said, grabbing the flash drive and stuffing it into my pocket.

We sprinted out of the room, weaving through the corridors as guards flooded the area, their voices shouting orders as they searched for us. We ducked into a maintenance tunnel, using the map to guide us toward the exit. The air was thick with tension, every step echoing in the confined space as we ran, our hearts pounding in our chests.

As we neared the exit, we encountered a final checkpoint—a pair of guards blocking our path. Lena and I exchanged a look, nodding in silent agreement. We moved as one, taking down the guards with swift, precise movements, our years of training coming into play.

With the guards subdued, we slipped past the checkpoint and into the final corridor leading to the exit. The door loomed ahead, a sliver of light visible through the cracks, promising freedom on the other side.

Just as we reached the door, a group of soldiers rounded the corner, their weapons raised.

"Freeze!" one of them shouted, his voice laced with authority.

Lena and I exchanged a glance, and without hesitation, we burst through the door, running out into the open. Alarms blared behind us, and we could hear the soldiers giving chase, their footsteps pounding as they closed in.

But we didn't stop. We ran with everything we had, disappearing into the shadows of the facility's exterior, blending into the maze of alleys and side streets that surrounded the compound.

As we escaped into the night, the weight of what we'd learned pressed down on us. Hitler's forces were preparing to invade Earth, and they had the technology, the resources, and the determination to make it happen.

But we had something they didn't: knowledge.

And we were going to use it to stop them.

Chapter 8: A Desperate Warning

The path to the Stargate room was harrowing, each step filled with the weight of impending disaster. Lena and I moved as quickly and quietly as we could, ducking into dark corners and hidden alcoves whenever a guard or soldier crossed our path. The sound of alarms still echoed faintly in the background, but as we approached the heart of the compound, a tense silence settled around us, punctuated only by the hum of machinery and the occasional click of boots on metal floors.

Finally, we reached the corridor that led to the Stargate room. I halted, gripping Lena's arm as I peered around the corner. My breath caught at the sight that greeted me. The entrance to the Stargate was heavily guarded by elite soldiers, their uniforms and weapons gleaming under the harsh fluorescent lights. High-ranking officers stood among them, their posture rigid, their expressions severe. This wasn't just a checkpoint; it was a fortress.

"Of course they'd have it heavily guarded," I whispered, feeling the weight of the situation pressing down on me. "They know how valuable this technology is."

Lena leaned in, her face pale but resolute. "We have to get through them, Ethan. We don't have a choice. Earth needs to know what's coming, and we're the only ones who can warn them."

I nodded, steeling myself. "We'll need to create a distraction, something that'll draw their attention away from the door just long enough for us to slip in."

She scanned the area, her eyes sharp. "There's a control panel over there, near the far wall. If we could overload it, it might buy us a few moments."

Without another word, we moved carefully across the corridor, keeping low and staying out of sight. I reached the control panel and quickly assessed its layout. It was a standard power junction, likely controlling the lights and temperature of the immediate area. With a few precise tweaks, I could overload it.

I glanced at Lena, giving her a quick nod. She braced herself, ready to make a run for the Stargate door as soon as the distraction kicked in.

Taking a deep breath, I pulled a wire and twisted it with another, causing a sharp spark that sent the lights flickering overhead. The hum of machinery grew louder, and then, with a loud pop, the panel emitted a small explosion, sending a cascade of sparks into the air. The guards and officers turned, startled by the sudden malfunction.

"Now!" I whispered, grabbing Lena's hand as we darted toward the door.

We slipped past the confused guards, pressing ourselves against the walls as we moved swiftly and silently. With a quick, precise motion, I entered the access code Lukas had provided into the control pad by the door. The door slid open, and we slipped inside, holding our breath as it closed behind us with a soft hiss.

The Stargate room was vast and imposing, a cavernous space filled with cables, machinery, and towering computer consoles. In the center of the room stood the Stargate itself, a massive, circular device surrounded by a ring of shimmering metal. Its surface pulsed with an otherworldly glow, casting an eerie light across the room. The sight of it was both awe-inspiring and terrifying.

Lena and I approached the control console, our hearts pounding. "If we can configure the Stargate to send a signal through to Earth, maybe we can warn them about the invasion," she whispered, her fingers hovering over the controls.

I nodded, feeling a mixture of fear and hope. "Let's make it quick. We don't have much time before someone realizes we're in here."

Lena worked swiftly, her hands moving over the console with practiced ease as she configured the settings. I watched the Stargate, its surface beginning to ripple and pulse in response to her adjustments.

The machinery around us hummed, and the portal started to emit a faint glow, brighter than before. It was working.

But just as we were about to initiate the signal, the door to the room slid open with a menacing hiss. I whipped around to see Dr. Weiss standing in the doorway, flanked by two guards. Her expression was cold, her eyes filled with a dangerous gleam.

"What do you think you're doing?" she demanded, her voice sharp and accusatory.

Lena and I exchanged a quick, panicked glance, but I forced myself to stay calm. "We're trying to prevent a catastrophe, Dr. Weiss," I said, stepping forward. "You know what Hitler plans to do. If he invades Earth, millions of lives will be lost."

Dr. Weiss's expression didn't soften. If anything, her gaze grew colder. "You're interfering with a mission that's been decades in the making, Dr. Cole. The Führer's vision is for a world free from the Controllers' manipulation—a world where humanity is free. You'd understand if you weren't so blinded by your limited perspective."

Her words sent a chill down my spine, but I forced myself to focus. "You don't understand, Dr. Weiss. Hitler's not planning liberation; he's planning domination. He wants control, not freedom. And Earth will suffer for it."

She raised an eyebrow, her mouth twisting into a faint smirk. "And who are you to judge what's best for humanity, Dr. Cole? We've lived in the shadows of falsehoods and restrictions for too long. The Fourth Reich is humanity's only chance for true freedom."

Lena took a step forward, her voice laced with anger. "This isn't freedom. It's oppression, the same kind of control you claim to despise. You're just replacing one tyrant with another."

Dr. Weiss's face hardened. "Enough," she snapped. She motioned to the guards, who stepped forward, their hands resting on their weapons.

I glanced at Lena, silently signaling her to be ready. We were cornered, but I wasn't about to let Dr. Weiss stop us. Taking a deep breath, I reached for the control panel and hit the activation sequence.

The Stargate flared to life, the portal shimmering as it stabilized. A soft, pulsing light filled the room, casting strange shadows across the walls. I watched as the signal indicator blinked, showing that a transmission was beginning.

Dr. Weiss's eyes widened as she realized what I'd done. "Stop them!" she barked, her voice filled with rage.

The guards rushed forward, but Lena and I moved quickly, positioning ourselves defensively. I tried to buy us a few more seconds, pressing buttons to send as much data through the portal as possible. "If we can just get a message out," I muttered, focusing on the controls.

But before I could finish, one of the guards grabbed Lena, wrenching her away from the console. She struggled, but he held her firmly. Another guard moved toward me, forcing me away from the controls, but not before I managed to press the final transmission button.

The portal shimmered, sending a fragmented, garbled message through before it began to destabilize. I didn't know if the message would be clear, but at least something was going through—some kind of warning.

Dr. Weiss approached, her face livid as she stared at me. "Do you realize what you've done?" she hissed, her voice trembling with fury. "You've jeopardized everything. The Führer's vision, the future of humanity—you've put it all at risk."

I met her gaze, refusing to back down. "No, Dr. Weiss. I'm protecting humanity. From people like you, who think control and domination are the answers. Earth deserves the chance to be free, not enslaved by another regime."

Her eyes flashed with anger, and for a moment, I thought she might strike me. But instead, she turned to the guards. "Take them.

Lock them up and make sure they're heavily guarded. They won't get another chance to interfere."

The guards grabbed Lena and me, dragging us toward the exit. I struggled against their grip, casting one last glance at the Stargate as it flickered and dimmed. The message had been sent, fragmented though it was. It was Earth's only chance to prepare, to stand a fighting chance against the invasion.

As the guards marched us out of the Stargate room, Lena shot me a grim, determined look. "At least we managed to get something through," she whispered, her voice barely audible.

I nodded, my heart heavy but resolute. "It's a start. But we're not done yet."

Dr. Weiss's voice echoed behind us as we were led away. "You've made a grave mistake, Dr. Cole. You've chosen the wrong side of history."

I didn't respond, but I held Lena's gaze, silently reassuring her. We'd made the right choice, even if it meant risking everything. And as we were led back down the sterile corridors, I knew one thing for certain.

We weren't giving up. Not yet.

Back in the confines of our cell, the weight of our actions settled over us. The guards had been instructed to watch us closely, their faces expressionless as they stood stationed by the door. Every time I glanced toward the Stargate, I felt a flicker of hope. Despite the fragmentary nature of our message, it was out there, a beacon to whoever might receive it on Earth. We could only hope it would reach someone who could make sense of it in time.

Lena paced the cell, her expression tense. "Do you think it got through?"

I nodded, though I wasn't sure. "It's hard to say. But at least there's a chance. Earth has to know what's coming, or they won't stand a chance against this invasion."

The minutes stretched into an eternity as we waited, every second bringing us closer to the impending assault on Earth. We couldn't do anything from within these walls, but we could hope—and we could plan.

Chapter 9: The Invasion Begins

The events of that day would be etched into my memory forever, each detail sharper and more harrowing than the last. As the weight of our failed warning pressed down on us, Lena and I could only wait, helpless, as the nightmare we'd tried to prevent began to unfold.

On Earth, thousands of miles away, a ripple of unease spread through the corridors of power. Deep within the halls of NASA, scientists gathered around flickering monitors, their faces bathed in the eerie blue glow of faint, erratic energy readings. It was subtle at first, almost imperceptible, but the readings were unusual enough to raise alarms. From a small control room at NASA's headquarters, analysts scrambled to understand the bizarre signals that seemed to be appearing out of nowhere, all pointing to an origin deep in the Arctic Circle, near a massive ice wall.

"Is it a solar flare?" one technician asked, his brow furrowed as he watched the data spike across the screen.

"No," another responded, shaking her head. "The pattern is too erratic, too... artificial. It's almost like..." She trailed off, unwilling to finish her thought.

"Like a portal," murmured Dr. Emerson, a senior physicist, who had been called in to examine the data. He spoke the word with a mixture of awe and disbelief. His colleagues turned to him, eyes wide with a mixture of curiosity and dread. For years, whispers of conspiracy theories and hidden realms had persisted among fringe communities, but to see something so close to those fantasies in real-time was unsettling.

As more readings poured in, it became clear this wasn't an isolated incident. The energy signatures continued to grow in strength, suggesting something monumental was building—a power source unlike anything they'd seen before. Soon, the intelligence community was alerted, and agencies worldwide were informed of the strange activity emanating from the Arctic region. Confusion spread like wildfire, with government officials exchanging terse messages, scrambling to understand the nature of the threat.

In Washington, D.C., the Pentagon held an emergency meeting, where generals, scientists, and intelligence officials gathered in a dimly lit war room, their faces tense and grave. Satellite images projected onto the wall showed strange fluctuations near the Arctic Circle, along with faint, ominous signals detected by ground stations.

"What exactly are we looking at here?" General Matthews demanded, his grizzled face a mask of steely resolve.

Dr. Porter, a top scientist from NASA, took a deep breath before speaking. "We're not entirely sure, but the signals suggest a massive energy disturbance—something that could be consistent with a large-scale dimensional rift."

"A dimensional rift?" one of the generals scoffed, disbelief coloring his voice. "Are you saying this is... some kind of portal?"

"Not just any portal," Dr. Porter replied grimly. "If our data is correct, this could be a gateway—something that can transport matter on a scale we've never seen before. And if that's true... we may be facing a threat unlike anything in human history."

The room fell silent as everyone absorbed the gravity of his words. A quiet tension hung in the air as officials struggled to reconcile the impossible with reality.

"We need to prepare," General Matthews said, breaking the silence. "Whatever this is, we can't be caught off guard. Mobilize all available forces and keep monitoring the situation. I want updates every ten minutes. And, God help us... let's hope we're wrong."

Back in Area 50, the atmosphere was electric with anticipation. Hitler and his top generals gathered in the main hall, where the Stargate stood tall and foreboding, its surface rippling with a sinister, pulsating glow. A faint hum filled the room, growing louder with each passing second as the machine powered up, its energy feeding into a storm of crackling electricity.

Lena and I had been positioned in a corner, shackled and watched by guards, our hearts pounding as we watched the unfolding spectacle. Despite the restraints, we strained forward, desperate to understand what was happening. Our captors kept us under close surveillance, ensuring we couldn't interfere.

Hitler himself stood before the Stargate, his frail frame casting a shadow against the towering device. Despite his age, there was a feverish gleam in his eyes—a man who saw his vision finally coming to life. Around him, his generals were solemn, their expressions a mixture of reverence and resolve. They believed in this mission, in the twisted promise of a Fourth Reich reborn, and they were prepared to die for it.

The Stargate's glow intensified, filling the room with a brilliant, unnatural light. Hitler raised a hand, and the room fell silent. His voice, though weakened by age, held a commanding presence.

"Today," he began, his words slow and deliberate, "we reclaim our place in history. We have waited in the shadows for too long, watching as the Controllers and their puppets spread their lies, distorting the truth of our world. But today, we take our first steps back into the world that is rightfully ours."

The soldiers and officers in the room stood at attention, their faces hard, unwavering. There was no doubt, no fear—only blind loyalty to a man they believed to be their savior.

Hitler gestured to his generals, who nodded in unison, each preparing to lead his troops through the portal. Rows of soldiers, equipped with advanced weaponry and armored vehicles, lined up before the Stargate, waiting for the signal.

"Go forth," Hitler commanded, his voice echoing through the chamber. "Bring order to a world steeped in chaos. Show them the power of the Reich."

With a roar of approval, the first line of soldiers marched toward the Stargate, their faces expressionless, eyes fixed on the shimmering portal. The soldiers moved with the precision of a well-oiled machine, stepping through the gate and disappearing in flashes of light. Armored vehicles followed, their engines growling as they rumbled toward the portal, vanishing into the void one by one.

I could only watch, horror gripping my heart, as I realized the scale of their forces. Hundreds—no, thousands—of soldiers, each outfitted with technology that far surpassed anything Earth's militaries could hope to match. And they were just the beginning.

Lena squeezed my hand, her face pale, her eyes wide with terror. "This is really happening," she whispered, her voice barely audible. "They're actually going to invade Earth."

I swallowed, my throat dry. "We have to find a way to stop them, Lena. Somehow."

But deep down, a part of me feared it was already too late.

The invasion was meticulously coordinated, a strike that targeted Earth's most powerful nations in a single, devastating blow. In Berlin, New York, Moscow, and London, the night sky lit up with the sudden appearance of dark, sleek aircraft that seemed to materialize out of thin air. Cloaked in technology that rendered them nearly invisible to radar, the Nazi forces struck with brutal precision, catching the world off guard.

In Berlin, civilians looked up in horror as beams of searing light rained down from the sky, obliterating key buildings and government centers. Explosions rocked the city, filling the air with the acrid scent of smoke and burning metal. Panic spread through the streets as people ran, their screams drowned out by the deafening roar of engines overhead.

Across the Atlantic, New York City faced a similar assault. High above Manhattan, Nazi aircraft hovered like dark specters, their weapons trained on the city below. In an instant, the Empire State

Building was engulfed in flames, its spire collapsing in a shower of debris. Skyscrapers crumbled, streets buckled, and chaos erupted as the invaders unleashed a fury that hadn't been seen since the darkest days of human conflict.

In Moscow, military bases were the first targets. Russian soldiers scrambled to defend their homeland, but the enemy's advanced technology overwhelmed them. Tanks exploded, planes were shot down, and soldiers fell in droves as the Nazi forces pressed forward, carving a path of destruction through the heart of the city.

And in London, Big Ben tolled its final hour as Nazi aircraft circled the city like vultures, striking down any resistance with merciless efficiency. The city's historic landmarks fell one by one, symbols of defiance reduced to rubble in a matter of minutes.

Back in Area 50, Lena and I stood helplessly, watching as wave after wave of soldiers and machines disappeared through the Stargate. The horror of it was almost too much to bear—the knowledge that Earth was under attack, that people were dying by the thousands, and that we could do nothing to stop it.

The room was filled with the sounds of machinery and the hum of the Stargate, but beneath it all, I could hear the faint echoes of gunfire and explosions coming through the portal. It was like a nightmare come to life.

"Ethan," Lena whispered, her voice choked with emotion. "They're going to destroy everything."

I clenched my fists, my body trembling with rage and helplessness. "We have to find a way to shut down the Stargate, Lena. If we can close it, we might be able to stop the invasion."

"But how?" she asked, desperation clear in her voice. "We're locked up, unarmed, and surrounded by guards. They'd never let us get close enough to the controls."

I knew she was right, but I refused to accept it. "We'll figure something out. We have to. We can't just stand here and watch as they tear our world apart."

Just then, the guards turned their attention to us, their faces blank and unfeeling. Hitler's plan was in motion, and we were little more than helpless spectators. But as the guards led us away from the Stargate, I couldn't shake the feeling that our moment was coming. We just had to be ready to seize it.

As we were escorted back to our quarters, the sounds of the invasion echoed in my mind, filling me with a determination that burned hotter than fear. This wasn't over—not yet.

Chapter 10: Fighting Back

The invasion unfolded with terrifying speed, as if the Nazis had perfected the art of coordinated chaos. Across the globe, Earth's major cities lay under siege, each targeted with a ruthless efficiency that left even the most prepared defenses scrambling in confusion. Cloaked aircraft and drones tore through the sky, undetected by radar, swooping down to release volleys of devastating fire on government buildings, media stations, and power grids. The invaders seemed to know exactly where to strike, hitting Earth where it was most vulnerable.

In Washington, D.C., the White House was a fortress of organized panic, its halls filled with the frantic sounds of hurried commands and desperate voices. Military leaders and government officials darted through the corridors, communicating with defense stations across the country. The attack had been swift and unpredictable, catching everyone off guard.

"Status report on New York!" General Matthews barked, his face a mask of barely controlled anger as he paced in front of a large digital map displaying real-time updates.

An officer looked up, his face pale. "Sir, the invaders have targeted key infrastructure—power plants, transportation hubs, media stations. Our forces are mobilizing, but the cloaking technology makes it difficult to locate and track their aircraft."

General Matthews cursed under his breath. "Keep trying. We need to establish a visual, or we're shooting in the dark."

Meanwhile, civilians poured out into the streets, wide-eyed with fear as they looked up at the sky, where the sleek, silent aircraft hovered like dark clouds. As the invaders struck at power grids, entire neighborhoods were plunged into darkness, their only illumination the eerie red glow of distant fires and the occasional flash of light from explosions. The once-bustling cities were now war zones, and people could only run, seeking shelter where there was none.

In Berlin, the echoes of the invasion reverberated in a way that felt almost poetic, like history being twisted back on itself. Nazi forces bombarded the very place where the Third Reich had risen and fallen, obliterating its landmarks as though rewriting the story they thought they owned. The people of Berlin resisted fiercely, their resolve unyielding despite the carnage around them. Makeshift militias formed, civilians arming themselves to defend their homes, their families, their history.

"Stay back!" an old man shouted in German, gripping a battered rifle as he led a group of locals to barricade a street corner. "They want to take our city, but we won't let them have it."

Across the world, resistance was mounting, but the odds were grim. The invaders' technology was leagues ahead, and their attacks came with the precision of a long-honed plan. Armies scrambled to defend their homelands, only to be blindsided by drones that swooped in silently, striking with unrelenting force. It was a modern-day blitzkrieg, an attack calculated to sow fear, chaos, and submission.

Back in Area 50, Lena and I watched the destruction with horror and guilt. The sounds of our world falling apart were more than we could bear, each explosion and scream from the portal twisting in my gut like a knife. We had tried to warn them, to do something—anything—to prevent this. But now, we were left with only one option.

"We have to sabotage the Stargate," I said, my voice steady, though my heart pounded with fear. "If we can disable it, we can cut off their connection to Earth."

Lena nodded, her face tense. "But how? This place is crawling with guards, and the Stargate is surrounded by soldiers. We'll never get close enough without being caught."

I thought for a moment, my mind racing. "We need an insider—someone who knows how the Stargate works and has access to its control system."

Before Lena could respond, the door swung open, and Dr. Weiss entered the room. Her face was as impassive as ever, but there was a flicker of something in her eyes that hadn't been there before—doubt, perhaps, or even guilt.

"Dr. Weiss," I said cautiously, trying to gauge her intentions. "Come to gloat?"

She ignored my jab, her gaze fixed on us with a grim intensity. "I know what you're planning, Dr. Cole," she said. "And while I may not agree with your methods, I... understand your reasoning."

Lena stiffened beside me, her eyes narrowing. "Understand? You're helping Hitler invade Earth. You're responsible for all of this!"

Dr. Weiss flinched slightly, but her composure remained intact. "You don't understand. I've devoted my life to scientific advancement, to unlocking the mysteries of the universe. But I didn't sign up for... this," she said, gesturing to the portal, where Nazi forces continued to pour through, their faces cold and unfeeling.

I took a cautious step forward, sensing an opportunity. "Then help us stop it. Help us shut down the Stargate before it's too late."

She hesitated, glancing at the portal, then back at us. "It won't be easy," she said finally, her voice low. "But you're right. If this invasion succeeds, it won't just be Earth that suffers—it'll be humanity, all over again. And I won't be a part of it."

A flicker of relief washed over me. "What do we need to do?"

Dr. Weiss drew a deep breath, her gaze steady. "The Stargate's controls are highly encrypted, but I have access to the system. If we can reach the control room undetected, I might be able to destabilize the portal long enough to disrupt the connection."

Lena glanced at me, her face a mixture of hope and skepticism. "And you're sure you're not just trying to lead us into another trap?"

Dr. Weiss met her gaze with surprising frankness. "I may have made mistakes, but I have no interest in seeing Earth fall to ruin. I'll help you. But we have to act quickly."

Chapter 11: The Heart of the Reich

The stakes had never felt higher. As we descended deeper into the heart of Area 50, each step felt heavier, like the facility itself was tightening around us. The shadows seemed to watch our every move, and the cold, industrial air pressed in, suffocating in its silence. But turning back was no longer an option. We had come too far, and the threat of Hitler's vision extending to Earth was unthinkable. We had to stop it—no matter the cost.

Dr. Weiss led the way, her movements quick and methodical as she guided us through a maze of hidden corridors. She'd revealed critical access points—shadowed alcoves and long-forgotten service passages that few guards knew existed. Her intimate knowledge of the facility was our only shield, the one advantage we had in this grim place.

"Are you sure these passages are clear?" Lena whispered, glancing over her shoulder, her breath shallow.

Dr. Weiss nodded, her expression tight. "These areas are rarely patrolled. Stick close. If we're quiet and quick, we'll reach the Stargate control room without alerting anyone."

The air was thick with tension as we advanced. The walls seemed to narrow around us, and every echo of footsteps, every distant clang, felt amplified, sharpening our senses. Each pause felt like a fragile moment on the edge, where the wrong move would expose us and undo everything.

When we reached a security checkpoint—a barrier with two armed guards stationed on either side—Dr. Weiss motioned for us to duck behind a stack of large metal crates. Her gaze turned calculating, cold.

"There's a service hatch to the ventilation system on the other side," she murmured. "If I distract them, you can slip past."

I glanced at Lena, who nodded, though her face showed her unease. "It's too dangerous, Dr. Weiss."

She met my gaze, unflinching. "I know my role. When I signal, move fast."

Dr. Weiss stepped out from behind the crates, her voice calm but authoritative as she addressed the guards. Her commands sounded genuine, holding their attention, their eyes locked on her.

"Now!" she hissed, gesturing for us.

We moved in tandem, darting past the guards to the service hatch. The moment we were through, I helped Lena pull the hatch shut. Moments later, Dr. Weiss slipped in beside us, her breathing heavy but controlled. Her face was taut with tension, a reminder of the stakes we faced with every step.

The corridors grew tighter as we approached the last checkpoint before the control room. The air seemed to thicken, every breath charged with the dread of what lay ahead. Dr. Weiss's face took on a hard, determined expression, her resolve unwavering as she stopped in front of a reinforced door.

"Once we're inside, I'll access the Stargate's mainframe," she whispered. "Destabilizing the portal could set off alarms, so be prepared."

I nodded, gripping her shoulder briefly. "We'll handle whatever comes. Just get us that opening."

Dr. Weiss punched a code into the panel, and the door slid open with a quiet hiss, revealing a room buzzing with electronics. Cables sprawled across the floor like veins, connecting the flickering monitors to the ominously humming control console at the room's center. The console's screens flashed with streams of data, the Stargate's readings fluctuating in ominous waves.

Dr. Weiss moved to the console, her fingers flying over the keys with practiced ease. Lena and I stood guard, every passing second feeling like a countdown to disaster.

"Almost there," Dr. Weiss muttered, her voice barely audible. "Just a few adjustments—"

Suddenly, an alarm blared, a flashing red light strobing through the room. Within seconds, guards stormed in, their weapons raised. Lena and I reacted instinctively, clashing with them in a desperate struggle, the noise of combat echoing in the confined space.

"Hurry, Dr. Weiss!" I shouted, dodging a guard's strike, my muscles burning with the effort to hold them off.

"I'm almost there!" she replied, her tone fierce as she kept working, her hands steady.

A low hum emanated from the console as the portal flickered, its glow dimming as the stabilizers began to collapse. Dr. Weiss looked up, triumph flashing in her eyes.

"It's done! They won't be able to sustain the portal for long."

But before relief could sink in, a gunshot rang out. Dr. Weiss stumbled, clutching her side, blood seeping between her fingers. She looked at me, her face softening, resignation in her eyes.

"Go," she whispered, her voice barely a breath. "Stop them. Don't let this sacrifice be in vain."

Her body crumpled, the life fading from her eyes. Lena let out a choked sound of grief, but there was no time to mourn. I pulled her forward, and we fled as the portal's glow sputtered, unstable and fading. A small victory—but we knew this wasn't over.

Bursting into the main control room, we found ourselves in a vast circular chamber, the air thick with the hum of powerful machinery. At the center stood the Stargate's master control panel, but before we could reach it, a line of elite soldiers, Hitler's personal guard, blocked our path. Clad in black, their faces hidden behind masks, their weapons gleamed with a deadly precision that sent a chill down my spine.

Lena tightened her grip on my arm, her voice a strained whisper. "We're outnumbered, Ethan. How do we get through?"

Images of Dr. Weiss flashed through my mind. Her sacrifice had bought us this chance, and I couldn't let it be for nothing. I steeled myself, pushing down my fear. "We fight. For her. For everyone."

We stepped forward, our presence drawing the soldiers' attention, and without a word, they attacked. The room erupted in a violent clash of gunfire, shouts, and the harsh sound of steel meeting flesh. Amidst the chaos, Lena and I fought with everything we had, our every movement driven by a desperate need to end this nightmare.

Through sheer force of will, we reached the control panel, battered but determined.

Standing before the Stargate's control console, I felt the weight of our mission settle heavily on my shoulders. This was the core, the heart of their entire operation. If I could overload the system, I could collapse the portal, cutting off the invasion before it could begin.

"Can you do it?" Lena asked, her voice tense, her gaze flickering between me and the guards regrouping in the room.

I nodded, though my hands were shaking. "If I recalibrate the frequency settings, I can destabilize the portal. But we'll have to move fast."

I worked quickly, my fingers flying over the controls, adjusting the settings as the portal pulsed, its light flickering in warning. Alarms blared, red lights flashing as more guards poured in, but Lena stood guard beside me, defiant, holding them off with an unyielding ferocity.

The console readings spiked, and the portal began to collapse in on itself. I grabbed Lena's hand, and together, we sprinted toward the exit as the facility shuddered, the walls trembling with the force of the portal's implosion.

A massive shockwave rippled through the room, throwing us to the ground. For a moment, silence blanketed everything. As the dust began to settle, I opened my eyes, my vision blurred, finding Lena beside me, bruised but alive. The Stargate was gone—nothing remained but a smoldering crater.

We had done it. The invasion had been thwarted.

But as footsteps echoed down the hall, we knew this wasn't the end. We were still trapped deep in enemy territory, surrounded by those who would do anything to avenge the collapse of their twisted dream. Yet for the first time, hope flickered within me. We had cut off the invasion, halted Hitler's perverse vision from reaching Earth.

Now, we just had to survive.

Chapter 12: The Collapse

The rumbling started almost immediately, a deep, resonant hum that shook the very bones of the facility. Alarms blared, their shrill cries echoing down the metallic corridors, signaling what we had both hoped for and feared: the Stargate's destabilization was triggering a full-blown containment breach. The countdown to the collapse had begun, and Lena and I were at its epicenter.

"Run!" I shouted, grabbing Lena's arm and pulling her forward just as the floor beneath us trembled with a violent jolt. The lights flickered erratically, casting the corridors into a dizzying mix of light and shadow. The energy from the overloaded Stargate pulsed through the walls, rattling pipes and panels loose, sending sparks showering down like hot rain.

We sprinted through the labyrinthine corridors, the wail of the alarms almost deafening. Red emergency lights painted the walls with an ominous glow, casting long, jagged shadows that stretched and warped with each turn we took. Lena matched my pace, her face pale but resolute, her breaths ragged as we navigated the chaos.

"The whole place is coming down!" she gasped, her voice barely audible over the alarms.

"Good," I said through gritted teeth. "With any luck, we'll take the Fourth Reich down with it."

But as we rounded a corner, a squad of guards appeared, blocking our path with weapons drawn. Their faces were steeled with anger, their stances unwavering. There was no time to hide, no time to retreat. I threw a desperate glance around, spotting a narrow side corridor to our right.

"This way!" I shouted, pushing Lena ahead of me. We ducked into the corridor, skidding around corners as the guards' shouts and footsteps echoed behind us.

Another tremor shook the ground, this one stronger, sending us stumbling into the walls. The containment breach was accelerating, its force growing with every passing second.

"Do you have any idea where we're going?" Lena asked, glancing at me as we ran.

"Not really," I admitted. "But we need to put as much distance between us and the Stargate as possible. The energy build-up is only going to get worse."

We could hear the escalating roar of the Stargate's instability echoing through the facility, each pulse stronger and more destructive than the last. Just as we reached what looked like an exit corridor, a blast of light flared from behind us, followed by a deafening explosion. The shockwave slammed into us, knocking us both off our feet and sending us tumbling forward.

The sound was overwhelming, a cacophony of metal twisting, walls shattering, and machinery imploding under the force of the blast. I braced myself, covering my head as chunks of debris rained down around us, the floor trembling beneath us like an earthquake. Lena lay beside me, her face pale as she shielded herself from the debris.

When the roar subsided, I forced myself to my knees, my vision swimming. I looked behind us, and my breath caught in my throat. The entire corridor we had just come through was a smoldering ruin, the walls caved in, the floor littered with chunks of metal and exposed wiring. The energy from the Stargate had torn through the facility, its power consuming everything in its path.

"We have to keep moving," I whispered, reaching out to help Lena to her feet.

We staggered forward, our movements sluggish as we stumbled through the last few corridors that led to the exterior of the facility. The explosions continued behind us, each one more powerful than the last, sending shockwaves that rippled through the walls and threatened to collapse the entire structure.

Finally, we saw a faint light up ahead—the facility's main exit. Gathering the last of our strength, we sprinted toward it, feeling the heat and pressure of the explosion closing in from behind.

Just as we burst through the doors, a massive explosion tore through the facility, the ground beneath us quaking as the Stargate collapsed in on itself. We were thrown forward by the force of the blast, landing hard on the barren terrain outside. I coughed, choking on the dust and smoke that billowed out from the ruined facility.

I looked up, my heart pounding as I took in the sight before us. The facility was engulfed in flames, parts of it crumbling as the Stargate's energy continued to consume it from within. Thick clouds of smoke rose into the air, blotting out the sky, and a hot, acrid wind whipped through the barren landscape.

Lena lay beside me, her face streaked with dirt but alive, her eyes wide as she took in the destruction we had unleashed. "We did it," she whispered, a mixture of relief and horror in her voice. "We actually did it."

But our victory was short-lived.

It didn't take long for word of our sabotage to reach Hitler. As Lena and I struggled to regain our breath, the faint sound of distant shouting reached our ears, followed by the rumble of approaching vehicles. We both froze, exchanging a horrified glance as we realized what was happening.

"They're coming for us," Lena said, her voice barely audible.

In the distance, we could see soldiers pouring out of nearby outposts, mobilizing with a fury that was palpable even from where we stood. Trucks, armored vehicles, and motorcycles formed a growing wave as they sped toward us, each one emblazoned with the twisted insignias of the Fourth Reich. There was no mistaking their purpose. Hitler had unleashed his forces with one objective: to hunt us down and kill us.

The faint crackle of a loudspeaker echoed across the barren landscape, followed by a voice that chilled me to the core. Hitler's voice, raspy and filled with venom, rang out, reaching us even from a distance.

"Dr. Cole," he began, his tone laced with unrestrained fury. "You have defied the Reich, and you will suffer the consequences. You thought you could stop us, but you have only delayed the inevitable. You and your accomplice have nowhere to run. I will find you, and when I do, you will know the true meaning of suffering."

The loudspeaker crackled, then went silent, leaving an oppressive stillness in its wake. Lena and I stood there, our hearts racing, as we took in the gravity of our situation. We were fugitives, hunted by one of the most dangerous forces imaginable, trapped in a desolate land with limited resources and nowhere to hide.

"We need to move," I said, my voice shaking as I forced myself to focus. "They'll be on us in minutes."

Lena nodded, her face pale but resolute. "Then let's go. We've made it this far. We're not giving up now."

We turned, sprinting across the barren terrain, our footsteps kicking up clouds of dust as we put as much distance as possible between us and the approaching forces. The landscape stretched out before us, an expanse of dry earth and jagged rocks that offered little cover, but we kept moving, our only hope lying in the possibility of escape.

Behind us, the sounds of engines and shouting grew louder, closer, as Hitler's forces closed in. The adrenaline surged through my veins, fueling my movements as I pushed forward, desperate to stay ahead of the relentless tide of soldiers and vehicles.

As we ran, I couldn't help but think about the consequences of our actions. We had succeeded in stopping the invasion, but at a cost that now seemed insurmountable. Hitler's wrath was now focused solely on us, his determination to see us dead as strong as his vision for a world under his control.

A part of me wondered if we had made the right choice. But as I glanced at Lena, saw the resolve in her eyes, I knew that we had done what was necessary. The world would never know the danger it had been spared, the horrors we had prevented. But Lena and I knew. And as long as we were alive, we had to keep fighting.

The chase went on, the barren landscape offering little refuge as we fled across the desolate terrain. The sounds of Hitler's forces echoed around us, the roars of engines and shouts of soldiers filling the air as they pursued us with relentless determination.

But we kept running, driven by a singular purpose: survival.

As the sun dipped below the horizon, casting long shadows over the barren land, Lena and I pushed forward, our bodies aching, our breaths labored, but our resolve unbroken. We had faced death and destruction, betrayal and loss, but we were still here. And as long as we were, we would keep fighting.

Chapter 13: The Tide of Power

Hitler sat behind a dark, polished desk in his private quarters, a faint glow from the television screen casting eerie shadows across his face. His gaze was fixed on the screen, which displayed a series of rapid, chaotic images: scenes of crumbling cityscapes, smoke billowing from government buildings, and soldiers with swastikas emblazoned on their uniforms marching through streets around the world. This was his vision realized, the dream of the Reich spreading across Earth.

The faint echo of footsteps interrupted his reverie. Hitler's head snapped up as the door swung open, and General Reinhardt strode in, his posture rigid, his face a mask of tension.

"Führer," Reinhardt began, his voice as steady as he could muster, though a hint of unease lingered in his eyes.

Hitler's eyes narrowed as he gestured for Reinhardt to speak. "General, what news do you bring?"

Reinhardt stepped forward, his voice low but clear. "Führer, we have a problem. Our forces in Area 51 are advancing as planned, and we're holding control over the initial cities of the Earth. However, the resistance on their side is stronger than anticipated. Their defenses are mounting, and our current forces may not be enough to secure all the territories."

Hitler's eyes flashed with anger. "Are you telling me that despite everything we've prepared for, our victory is not yet assured?"

Reinhardt swallowed, maintaining his composure. "The initial strike was effective, Führer, but we require reinforcements if we are to expand and maintain control over all strategic points. Our forces in Area 50 are equipped and trained, but they are limited. We need more... power."

Hitler's gaze darkened, and he clenched his hands into fists. "Reinhardt, I did not come this far to hear excuses. The world is watching as the Reich reclaims its power. The people of Earth are witnessing the strength of our vision. Yet you tell me we risk losing it all due to insufficient reinforcements?"

"Führer," Reinhardt replied, a note of urgency in his tone, "we still have our connection to Area 51. Our forces there are in place, and they control key locations. But without immediate reinforcements from Area 50, we risk a substantial resistance that could undermine our entire operation. The Americans, the Russians, the English... they're all scrambling to fight back. If we do not act quickly, they may rally together, and—"

Hitler cut him off with a glare. "I have seen the might of our technology, Reinhardt! You know as well as I that the will of the Reich is unstoppable. We are not dealing with minor uprisings—we are dealing with a world that has grown weak, corrupt, and decadent under the influence of the Controllers and their puppets."

Reinhardt nodded, his voice steady. "Yes, Führer. And that is why I recommend we construct another Stargate immediately. We can establish a stronger, more permanent connection to Area 51 and beyond. With a continuous influx of our best forces, we will secure our hold and spread our reach even further."

Hitler's expression softened, and a twisted smile crept onto his face as he considered Reinhardt's suggestion. "A second Stargate... You realize what you're proposing, Reinhardt. This is no simple task. Constructing a new gate requires energy, resources, and skilled engineers. But... if we succeed... the Reich would have unlimited access to Earth. Our forces would be unstoppable, a wave of power sweeping across every corner of their world."

Reinhardt straightened, confidence returning to his voice. "Exactly, Führer. The construction will demand time and resources, but it will secure our dominance. We have the technology, and we have the soldiers willing to die for the Reich's vision. If we act now, we can launch a second wave that will crush any remaining resistance."

Hitler's gaze returned to the television, where scenes of devastation played out like a twisted symphony of his triumph. Flames engulfed towering buildings, and smoke blotted out the skies of cities around the world. Soldiers moved in disciplined lines through streets littered with debris, their faces expressionless, their movements mechanical. Civilians were herded into squares, their eyes wide with fear as they watched the Reich's banners unfurl over their cities.

"The world looks upon our work, Reinhardt," Hitler murmured, almost to himself. "For so long, they have lied to themselves, hidden behind the illusion of freedom and peace. The Allies claimed victory in 1945, claimed to have destroyed the Reich and crushed its vision." He chuckled, a dry, humorless sound. "But they were fools. The Controllers are fools. They think they understand power. They think they can hold the reins of history. But they were mistaken."

Reinhardt watched Hitler intently, sensing the weight of his words.

"All this time," Hitler continued, his voice growing louder, "they thought they had silenced me. They believed I was gone, relegated to the annals of history, forgotten. But history cannot silence truth. The Reich will rise from the ashes of their lies, stronger and more powerful than ever. And this time, there will be no surrender."

The fury in his voice was palpable, a force that seemed to fill the room, pressing down on Reinhardt. He had seen Hitler's wrath before, but this was different. This was the voice of a man who had clawed his way back from defeat, a man who had defied the very forces of history itself.

Reinhardt's own resolve hardened in response. "Führer, I will personally oversee the construction of the new Stargate. We will establish a link that no one can sever. With your permission, we can begin immediately."

Hitler's eyes gleamed. "Yes. Begin the construction at once. We must not delay. And when the new Stargate is operational, we will launch an assault so devastating that Earth's leaders will kneel before us, begging for mercy."

A dark satisfaction settled over him, and he leaned back in his chair, his gaze never leaving the television screen. Images of destruction and chaos flashed before him, a visual testament to his revenge upon a world that had dared to defy him. He clasped his hands together, a small, twisted smile playing on his lips.

"Soon," he whispered, his voice filled with a mixture of menace and delight. "Soon, the Reich will rule every city, every land. There will be no safe haven for those who oppose us. Every soul on this Earth will know the name of Hitler, not as a shadow of the past, but as the architect of the future."

Reinhardt watched him, the general's own heart pounding with a mixture of fear and exhilaration. He had been by Hitler's side long enough to understand the man's drive, his unyielding will to dominate. And now, as they stood on the brink of realizing that vision, he felt the weight of their task settle over him like a shroud.

"Your orders will be carried out, Führer," Reinhardt said, his voice steady. "We will secure our hold on Earth. And with the second Stargate, there will be no limits."

Hitler nodded, his gaze shifting from the television to Reinhardt. "Go. Make it happen. Every moment wasted is a moment the enemy regroups. They may think they've tasted victory by stalling our forces. But they have only delayed the inevitable. And the Reich is nothing if not patient."

As Reinhardt turned to leave, Hitler's gaze returned to the screen, his voice dropping to a murmur as if speaking only to himself.

"The Controllers thought they could contain me. They thought they could control the truth, build a world on their lies. But they do not know true power. They have never faced the unyielding force of an idea that refuses to die."

He leaned forward, his eyes gleaming with malevolent pride. "Let them watch. Let them tremble. Every city that falls, every banner that flies with our symbol—it is a promise. A promise that history bends to the will of the strong, that destiny belongs to those who seize it with blood and fire."

His voice grew softer, as though savoring each word. "This time, there will be no treaties, no compromises. Only submission. The world will bow to us—or burn."

He allowed himself a rare moment of satisfaction, his gaze lingering on the images of destruction playing across the screen. Each city, each shattered landmark, was a testament to the resurgence of the Reich, a symbol of his triumph over the so-called victors of the last war.

Hitler's fingers tapped rhythmically on the desk, his mind already racing with plans for the next phase of the invasion. The new Stargate would be the key, a bridge between two worlds that would allow his forces to flow like an unstoppable tide.

The door clicked shut as Reinhardt left, and Hitler was alone once more, his twisted vision filling every corner of his mind. His gaze drifted to the skyline beyond the windows, a harsh, unyielding expanse of steel and power.

"They thought they had buried the Reich," he murmured, a small smile curving his lips. "But history has a way of repeating itself."

He reached out, his hand brushing against the cool surface of the television screen, as though caressing the flames that danced across it. His voice dropped to a whisper, filled with venomous resolve.

"And this time, we will not stop until every corner of this world knows the true meaning of power."

Chapter 14: Regrouping and Reflecting

I leaned back against the rough stone wall of the outpost, my chest heaving as I tried to catch my breath. Every muscle in my body ached, a reminder of the close calls and desperate escapes that had gotten us here. I looked over at Lena, who had slumped down beside me, her face pale but set with a hard resolve. Her eyes scanned the darkness outside our small hideout, vigilant and alert.

"We did it," she whispered, her voice barely louder than the wind whistling through the cracks in the stone. "We cut off the reinforcements. But... it's not enough, is it?"

I rubbed a hand over my face, feeling the grit and grime from the long trek through the wasteland. "No, Lena," I said, exhaling slowly. "It's not enough. Hitler's reach is still too vast, his followers too many. Cutting off one Stargate isn't going to dismantle the Fourth Reich. Not by a long shot."

A bitter silence hung between us, heavy and filled with the weight of our failure to truly end the threat. Yes, we had delayed him. Yes, we had prevented more soldiers from pouring through the portal, at least for now. But I'd seen the rage in Hitler's eyes, heard the absolute conviction in his voice. He wasn't going to let us get away with this. And he wasn't going to stop until he had the Earth under his boot once more.

I leaned forward, elbows on my knees, and stared out at the barren expanse that stretched out before us, desolate and unforgiving. The faint sounds of distant explosions and gunfire echoed in my mind, a grim reminder of the world we had left behind. Earth was still under siege, and it was only a matter of time before Hitler found another way to bring reinforcements to his side.

"Lena," I said softly, "have you thought about the Controllers?"

She turned to me, her brows furrowed in confusion. "The Controllers? You think they're involved in this?"

I nodded, my mind racing with possibilities, theories I hadn't dared to speak aloud until now. "Think about it. Hitler didn't just 'survive' all these years on his own. There's no way he could have orchestrated all of this alone. The technology, the resources... it's almost as if he was given a chance to escape, like he was placed here deliberately."

Lena frowned, her gaze sharpening as she followed my line of thought. "You think the Controllers wanted him here? That they... allowed this?"

"It's a possibility," I replied, my voice tinged with frustration. "They control everything else, after all. Why not the remnants of the Third Reich? If they allowed Hitler to carve out his own world here in Area 50, they must have had a reason. Maybe they saw him as a useful piece in their game, a way to keep humanity in check, or a failsafe against... I don't know, any uprising against their control."

Lena's eyes hardened, a spark of anger flickering in their depths. "So, they're using him to keep the world under control. And all this suffering, all this destruction... it's just a part of their plan."

"Exactly." I gritted my teeth, my fists clenching involuntarily. "It's like everything I've worked for, everything I've believed in, was just a lie. Science, progress, the idea that humanity could chart its own course... if the Controllers are behind all of this, then none of it was real. We're just... puppets in their hands."

Lena's hand found mine, her grip strong and steady. "Then we fight back, Cole," she said, her voice fierce. "We keep fighting until we tear down every lie, until we expose every shadow they've hidden in. Earth isn't safe until we dismantle the Fourth Reich's hold completely. And if the Controllers are behind this, then we'll bring them down too."

Her conviction sparked something in me, a flicker of hope amidst the despair. I nodded, squeezing her hand. "You're right. We can't give up. Not now. But we need a plan."

A sound outside the outpost sent both of us into silence. The crunch of boots on gravel, the faint rustle of equipment. My heart pounded in my chest as Lena and I exchanged a look of dread. We both knew what this meant.

I drew a breath and mouthed to her, "Stay calm."

But the footsteps grew closer, louder, and before we could react, a flashlight beam pierced through a crack in the wall, casting an eerie glow inside our hiding spot. Shadows moved across the entryway, and we heard muffled voices speaking in low, urgent tones. The sound of metal scraping on metal told me they were preparing weapons.

"Come out," a voice commanded in heavily accented English. "We know you're in there, Dr. Cole. Lena. There's nowhere left to run."

Lena's hand tightened on mine, her pulse racing beneath my fingers. I forced myself to stay calm, to think. If we went out there, we were at their mercy. But staying hidden was no longer an option. I took a deep breath and glanced at Lena, giving her a small nod.

Together, we stepped out of the shadows, our hands raised in surrender. The soldiers stood there, their faces grim, their weapons trained on us. They wore the insignia of the Reich, their uniforms pristine, their expressions as cold and unyielding as steel.

"Take them," one of the soldiers barked, his eyes hard as he motioned for us to step forward. "The Führer wants them alive."

A murmur ran through the soldiers, a flicker of malice in their eyes as they approached us, securing our hands behind our backs with harsh efficiency. I gritted my teeth against the pain as the restraints bit into my wrists, feeling a surge of defiance rise within me even as they marched us out of the outpost.

The leader of the group, a tall, stern-looking man with a scar that ran down the length of his cheek, stepped in front of us, his gaze cold and calculating. He inspected us with a disdainful sneer before speaking.

"Consider yourselves lucky," he said, his voice dripping with contempt. "The Führer has decided you're worth keeping alive... for now. He wants you to suffer first. Says it will serve as an example to those who think they can defy the Reich."

I met his gaze, refusing to look away despite the anger and fear churning within me. "He can make me suffer all he wants," I said, my voice low but firm. "But this isn't over. And he knows it."

The officer chuckled darkly, his expression twisted with amusement. "We'll see how defiant you are after a few weeks in our cells, Dr. Cole. The Führer has plans for you... plans that I guarantee will make you beg for death."

Lena glared at him, her eyes blazing with fury. "We'll see about that," she spat. "We've seen enough of your 'plans' to know that they always fall apart. Just like they will this time."

The officer's smirk faded, replaced by a look of cold rage. He motioned to his men, and they shoved us forward, forcing us to march through the barren wasteland. Every step felt like a defeat, a bitter reminder of the danger we were up against. The adrenaline had faded, leaving only the raw ache of exhaustion, the weight of our situation pressing down on me like a physical force.

As we were led toward what I assumed was a holding cell somewhere within the compound, my mind churned with thoughts of escape, plans that formed and faded as quickly as they'd come. The odds were stacked against us. Hitler's forces were ruthless, his resources seemingly endless. And now, he had us exactly where he wanted us—under his thumb, prisoners in his twisted version of reality.

But even as the cold wind bit into my skin and the rough terrain scraped against my feet, I refused to let despair take hold. There had to be a way out. There was always a way out.

I glanced at Lena, whose face was set with the same determination I felt. She met my gaze, a spark of defiance in her eyes, and I knew that, whatever happened next, we were in this together.

And as we were marched deeper into the heart of Hitler's stronghold, a new resolve settled within me.

This wasn't the end. Not by a long shot.

We would find a way to escape. We would fight back. And somehow, we would bring an end to this nightmare—once and for all.

Chapter 15: Confrontation with Hitler

The steel doors groaned open, and I felt a pair of rough hands shove me forward. I stumbled, catching myself just before I hit the cold, unforgiving ground. Lena was beside me, her eyes unyielding, a fierce fire in her gaze as she looked up at the man seated on the raised platform before us.

Adolf Hitler sat in a high-backed chair, his pale, weathered face twisted into a smile that chilled me to the bone. His body was fragile, aged almost beyond recognition, but his eyes were sharp as steel, filled with a dark, fervent gleam that seemed to reach across the room. The silence around us was unnerving, thick with an unspoken threat, as though the air itself was waiting for him to speak.

I forced myself to stand tall, ignoring the countless guards who lined the walls, their gazes as cold and unfeeling as stone. Lena's hand brushed mine, a brief, silent gesture of solidarity, and I held her gaze, drawing strength from her courage.

"Well," Hitler said, his voice a raspy whisper that somehow cut through the silence like a blade, "look at the two of you. Heroes, rebels, visionaries..." His lips curled into a sneer. "Traitors."

The word landed like a stone in my stomach, the weight of it almost suffocating. But I held his gaze, refusing to let him see the fear that stirred within me.

"We did what had to be done," I replied, my voice steadier than I felt. "We stopped you from unleashing a reign of terror on Earth. Your vision is nothing but a nightmare."

Hitler laughed, a hollow, rattling sound that seemed to echo off the steel walls, chilling me to my core. "Ah, but you misunderstand, Dr. Cole. This nightmare, as you call it, is the path to freedom. The path to order." He leaned forward, his eyes narrowing with dark intensity. "You think I am a monster, a tyrant, but my vision is the only way forward. Humanity has proven, time and again, that it cannot govern itself. It has drowned in decadence, weakness, under the veil of lies spun by the Controllers."

My fists clenched, resisting the urge to shout. "You're no better than them. All you want is power—to force the world to bend to your will."

"Power?" he sneered, his gaze icy and calculating. "Do you truly think the Controllers allowed me to rise to power without their consent? They permitted it, Dr. Cole, because they knew I was strong enough to challenge them."

Lena scoffed, contempt dripping from her words. "So, you traded your soul for a chance at their table? You became their puppet for a taste of power?"

Hitler's eyes flashed with anger as he rose slowly from his chair, his frail body straightening, his voice sharp and venomous. "They thought they could use me as a pawn in their games. They believed they could manipulate me, bend me to their will. But I was not like the others. I refused to play by their rules, refused to become another cog in their machine of deception."

He began to pace, each step measured and deliberate, his voice gaining a sinister edge. "Do you know what the Allies did after the war, Dr. Cole? They seized control of Earth's governments, one by one, under the invisible hand of the Controllers. They built NASA to spin their web of deception, feeding the masses lies about planets, stars, a universe beyond, to keep them docile, compliant. Everything you know—it is a puppet show, designed to keep humanity in line."

Lena's jaw clenched, her gaze piercing him with disgust. "You're delusional. The world moved on from you, Hitler. We built something better, something free."

"Free?" His bitter laugh rang out, mocking and hollow. "You are all chained to an illusion of freedom, blind to the true chains that bind you. The masses are shackled, their minds clouded with lies, their spirits broken by a false sense of choice. I sought to shatter that illusion, to bring them true freedom through unity, through strength." His voice dropped to a venomous whisper. "But you... you destroyed my work. You spit on everything I built."

"All you've built is a legacy of terror," I retorted, anger flaring in my chest. "You twisted history, warped reality, and sacrificed innocent lives just to feed your own delusions of superiority."

"Superiority?" He stopped pacing and fixed me with a penetrating stare. "I built order from chaos. I brought discipline, purpose, a vision of unity to a world that would rather drown in its own filth. The weak despise me because I reveal their cowardice; the Controllers despise me because I refuse to kneel." He took a step closer, his eyes like dark, bottomless pits. "You are no hero, Dr. Cole. You are a puppet of the very forces you think you oppose."

I forced my voice to remain steady, refusing to let his words sink in. "Better a puppet than a monster who would destroy everything to satisfy his twisted sense of destiny."

His smile twisted into a sneer. "And that is why you will die."

The silence that followed was thick, suffocating. Hitler's gaze shifted to Lena, his eyes gleaming with malicious satisfaction. "You have defied me, Dr. Cole. And you..." He turned to Lena, his sneer deepening. "You have stood by him, aided him in his treachery. For that, you will both suffer."

Lena lifted her chin defiantly, her eyes fierce and unwavering. "We're not afraid of you. You might see yourself as invincible, but history will remember you for what you are—a tyrant, a monster."

Hitler chuckled, shaking his head. "History is written by the victors, my dear. And when I am finished, your names will be nothing but a faint whisper, erased from the annals of time."

He gestured to the guards, his expression growing colder. "Take them. Sentence them to the cellars. Let them experience suffering as the Reich sees fit. Let their bodies serve as a warning to any who would dare challenge the vision of unity."

The guards moved forward, their hands seizing our arms with unrelenting force. I struggled against them, my heart pounding with the realization of what he was condemning us to. He didn't just want us dead—he wanted us erased, our existence reduced to nothing more than a cautionary tale.

Lena's voice cut through the silence, strong and defiant. "You may kill us, but you'll never kill the truth. The world will see you for what you are—a dictator, a relic clinging to a past no one wants."

Hitler's eyes narrowed, and he leaned in close, his breath cold as he whispered, "Then let the truth die with you."

Straightening, he addressed his guards with chilling finality. "Break them. Starve them, humiliate them. And when they are broken, leave them for the rats. Let the earth itself consume their bodies, piece by piece, as a testament to those who dare defy the Reich."

A surge of nausea rose in my throat, but I forced myself to stay calm, to keep my expression neutral. He wanted to see us crumble, to strip us of every shred of hope. But I wouldn't give him that satisfaction.

As the guards dragged us from the room, his laughter echoed behind us, a twisted, mocking sound that seemed to burrow into my mind, impossible to shake. Just before the doors closed, he let out one final, chilling laugh, his voice cold and laced with unhinged certainty:

"I will do whatever it takes to maintain the Reich, even if it means sacrificing Earth itself. The Fourth Reich will spread across every corner of the true Earth. God placed us here for this purpose, and I will see His will done. There will be no place untouched by my power, no shadow too small to escape my reach."

His words, spoken with such terrifying conviction, felt like a curse. They left a dark mark on my soul, an ominous weight that settled deep, as though his twisted destiny was now etched into the very fabric of my mind. As we were led away, shackled and weary, his words echoed endlessly—a grim reminder that, for us, this seemed like the end of our battle.

But even in that despair, a small spark flickered. This might be the end of one chapter, but it was not the end of our fight.

Chapter 16: A Narrow Escape

The room was silent, save for the faint hum of the monitors casting a dim, eerie light over Hitler's face as he watched us with a look of cruel satisfaction. His eyes gleamed with a twisted pleasure, as though our suffering was a carefully orchestrated symphony he intended to savor. Behind him, screens flickered to life, showing his forces storming into Earth's cities. The scenes shifted, flashing across Berlin, London, New York, Moscow—each city overtaken by the iron grip of his resurrected Reich.

Pain surged through my arms as the guards twisted them behind my back, the restraints so tight my shoulders felt close to snapping. My vision blurred with exhaustion and agony, yet I couldn't tear my gaze from the screens. Seeing Earth's cities fall under the swastika's shadow was like watching my own worst nightmare unfold—a nightmare where I felt both fury and despair in equal measure.

Beside me, Lena hung in her bindings, her face pale but her eyes fierce. She glanced at me, and though we couldn't speak, the unspoken resolve between us was unmistakable: we would not let him break us. Not now. Not ever.

"Do you see, Dr. Cole?" Hitler's voice was thick with perverse satisfaction as he gestured toward the screens. His frail hand trembled with the weight of his conviction. "Do you see what we are creating? A world united under strength and purpose, cleansed of weakness. Earth will finally know true freedom—freedom from its own decadence."

Fighting the burning pain in my muscles, I forced myself to meet his gaze. "You're delusional if you think this is freedom. All you're doing is spreading terror, destroying lives."

"Lives?" He scoffed, a sneer twisting his lips. "You cling to that word as though it holds meaning. Lives without purpose are a waste. The people of Earth have been led like cattle from birth to death, under the lie of freedom spun by the Controllers and their democracies. I offer them something greater: purpose. Strength. Unity."

Lena raised her head, her voice hoarse but defiant. "Strength?" she spat. "Murdering innocents, brainwashing the world under your rule? You're nothing but a relic, Hitler. Your time has passed."

His eyes darkened as he leaned forward, his expression turning cold and dangerous. "You speak of relics, Lena, yet you fail to see. I am not merely a man—I am an idea, a force that cannot be erased. The world needs order, a guiding hand. And I will be that hand. I will be the architect of Earth's rebirth."

He gestured to the guards, his voice dropping to a venomous whisper. "Begin."

The guards tightened their grip, one forcing my head back while another wrapped something sharp and cold around my wrists. The bite of metal against my skin was excruciating, and I fought the urge to cry out. I wouldn't give him that satisfaction.

But then, just as the guard prepared to tighten the restraints further, a low, pulsing hum filled the room. It grew louder, resonating through the walls, mingling with the sudden crackle of energy blasts. I strained to look, adrenaline surging through me as the guards hesitated, exchanging uncertain glances.

Without warning, the door burst open in a blinding flash of light and smoke. The guards staggered back, blinded, and through the haze, figures moved with lethal precision, shadows against the light flooding the room.

The first thing I noticed was their green skin, glowing even in the dim light. The green-skinned fighters moved in coordinated attacks, their weapons releasing bursts of energy that tore through the Nazi guards with brutal efficiency. One by one, Hitler's forces fell, their bodies hitting the ground in lifeless heaps.

Amidst the chaos, a figure stepped forward, her movements fierce, her stance commanding. As the smoke cleared, I saw her face—Sarah.

"Dr. Cole, Lena!" she shouted, her voice cutting through the clamor as she fired at a guard who attempted to raise his weapon. "We're getting you out of here."

"Sarah!" Lena's voice was a mix of relief and shock. "How did you—"

"No time for questions," Sarah replied, her eyes fixed on the guards. She raised a small device, aiming it at the metal bindings around my wrists. A pulse of energy shot out, severing the restraints instantly, and a wave of relief washed over me. She freed Lena next, her gaze flicking toward the door.

"We need to move. Now."

But before we could escape, the screens flickered, and Hitler's face appeared on the largest one, twisted with rage as he watched us through the feed.

"Kill them!" he bellowed, his voice vibrating with fury. "Kill them all!"

More guards poured in from the hallways, weapons drawn, and the room erupted in chaos again. Sarah raised her blaster, firing rapid shots as she covered our escape. The green-skinned fighters moved around us, their bodies weaving through the guards with fluidity and precision. They fought with a fierce resolve, their every move a testament to the resistance Hitler's regime had tried so desperately to crush.

"Go!" Sarah yelled, pushing us toward the open door as she continued to fire over our heads. "We need to get out of here before he calls for reinforcements!"

We stumbled into the corridor, the sound of gunfire and shouting echoing behind us. I felt Lena's hand grip mine tightly as we navigated the maze of twisting hallways, our only guide the faint light ahead that signaled our escape.

But as we reached the main exit, more guards appeared, blocking our path, their faces set in grim determination. Sarah stepped forward, her blaster at the ready, but I could see the exhaustion in her eyes, the strain of battle weighing on her.

Then, as if by some miracle, a soft, shimmering light appeared in the corner of the room. It grew brighter, solidifying into a familiar, rippling form—the Stargate.

"Sarah!" I gasped, heart pounding. "You opened it!"

She nodded, her expression resolute. "I programmed it to activate as soon as we reached this point. This is our one shot. Let's go!"

With a final surge of strength, Sarah unleashed a barrage of fire, creating a brief opening. She motioned for us to move, and together, we ran toward the Stargate, its pulsing light casting strange shadows across the walls.

Behind us, Hitler's enraged voice blared through the speakers. "Do not let them escape! Kill them all! They will pay for this!"

The light of the Stargate beckoned us, and without hesitation, we plunged into the portal, the world around us dissolving into a vortex of colors and light.

As we passed through, I felt the familiar weightlessness, the strange pull of time and space stretching around us. Lena's hand held mine tightly, grounding me as we hurtled through the unknown. The light grew brighter, warmer, until it filled my vision completely.

Chapter 17: Shifting Loyalties

We emerged from the shimmering portal, the glow fading behind us as we stepped back onto familiar ground. The alien landscape of Area 50, with all its horrors, felt like a distant memory now as the humid air and dim lighting of Area 52 filled my senses. Still, the weight of everything we had witnessed lingered, heavy and unyielding.

Sarah was waiting for us, arms folded across her chest, her expression unreadable. "It's good to see you both still in one piece," she said with a faint smile, though her eyes held shadows. "But you have no idea how deep you've gotten yourselves in."

I glanced at Lena, whose face mirrored my exhaustion and the lingering shock of what we'd been through. "Sarah," I began, voice barely above a whisper, "we've seen... things we never imagined. Hitler, the Controllers, the Reptilians—"

Sarah held up a hand, cutting me off. "I already know. We've been receiving updates from some of the green-skinned operatives in Area 50. They risked their lives to send us what they could."

Lena's eyes widened. "So... you knew all along?"

Sarah nodded, her gaze intense. "We knew enough. We knew something dangerous was brewing there—that Hitler had not only survived but somehow amassed power to resurrect his twisted vision. The Controllers gave him a foothold, but they underestimate him. He's a wild card, even by their standards."

Her words hit me like a blow. While we thought we were exposing dark secrets, the truth had already been known by others who were fighting a much larger battle. I felt a sick pit form in my stomach.

As if reading my thoughts, Sarah gestured to a figure emerging from the shadows behind her. It was one of the green-skinned leaders—a man with solemn eyes and a deep scar cutting across his cheek. He held himself with a quiet strength, his expression both weary and wise.

"You have done much for our people," he said, his voice a low rumble. "Your resistance to the Reptilians, your efforts in Area 50—they did not go unnoticed. That is why we aided you." He paused, looking at us with a searching intensity. "But you must understand—we can only risk so much."

Lena stepped forward, her face set with fierce resolve. "You've risked more than we can ever repay. But we can't ignore what's happening now. Earth is under attack. We can't just walk away."

The green-skinned leader shook his head slowly. "Your world has been under attack long before you were born. The Controllers have had their claws in your governments, your resources, even the knowledge allowed to your people. The Reptilians have entrenched themselves in your most powerful institutions. This invasion you see now is only an extension of the control that has existed for centuries."

A heavy silence followed his words as the truth settled around us. Everything we thought we'd fought to prevent was already deeply rooted, hidden behind the veils of our own governments, media, education. A surge of helplessness ran through me.

"So... we should just give up?" I asked, my voice hollow. "Let them take over and accept it?"

"No," he said softly, his gaze unwavering. "Survival is your battle now. Only if you survive can you fight them. Sometimes, survival is the only victory you can achieve in a world as controlled as yours."

I looked at Lena, who was tight with frustration, her eyes shining with defiance. "We can't just abandon Earth," she insisted, her voice breaking. "We've seen what they're doing. We can't walk away from that."

The green-skinned leader's gaze softened as though he pitied us. "You think your world is different? That your people are immune to the Controllers' influence?" He shook his head. "They already control Earth. You are fighting against shadows, illusions of freedom. The difference now is that you've finally seen through the lie."

Sarah broke the silence, her voice steady. "Look, I get it. We're all on the same side, even if our goals aren't perfectly aligned. But the reality is, you two have made yourselves a target. You've angered the Controllers, the Reptilians, and now Hitler's forces. Staying here puts all of us at risk."

Lena's face softened, her shoulders slumping as Sarah's words sunk in. "So, what do we do?"

Sarah reached into her pocket, pulling out a small metallic device with a soft, pulsing blue glow at its center. "This is a communicator. It's designed to connect between realms. If you need us, use this. It will allow us to track your location and, if we can, provide assistance."

I took the device, feeling the cool metal in my hand. It felt oddly comforting, as though it were a lifeline in the shadowy world we had entered.

"One more thing." Sarah reached into her satchel, producing a device that took my breath away—a Stargate controller, an exact replica of the one we'd lost. "This is a one-way ticket. It's set to open portals to random locations. Use it only if you have no other choice."

I nodded, gratitude mixing with a hint of fear. "Thank you, Sarah."

Her smile was faint. "Just be careful with it. And don't stay anywhere too long. The Controllers have their ways."

The green-skinned leader stepped forward, his tone solemn. "We have given what we can. Our battle with the Reptilians requires all of our strength. We wish you well, but we cannot fight this battle for you."

Lena nodded, her face a mask of determination. "Thank you. For everything."

He inclined his head, then turned, fading back into the shadows, leaving us alone with Sarah. She motioned toward the Stargate device in my hand. "Go on. Use it. We'll be watching for your signal."

Lena and I exchanged a glance, the tension between us unspoken but heavy. I held up the Stargate device, feeling its familiar hum. The air shimmered as a portal began to form, its edges crackling with energy.

I felt the pull, the strange sensation of time and space bending around us.

Without another word, we stepped into the portal, letting its energy wash over us. The world shifted, colors and lights twisting and blending as we traveled through realms unknown. Then, as suddenly as it began, it stopped.

But this time, something felt different.

The familiar weightlessness faded, replaced by a chilling stillness. We emerged into... nothing. A void, absolute and impenetrable, surrounded us in every direction. There was no light, no air, no sensation—just an endless, oppressive darkness that pressed in on every side. My heart pounded, panic setting in as I tried to grasp where we were.

"Lena?" I whispered, my voice echoing eerily in the vast emptiness.

"I'm here," she replied, her voice tight. She reached for my hand, her touch grounding me in the midst of the void.

The silence around us was unlike anything I had ever felt, dense and heavy, as though it was swallowing even the faintest sound. No sky, no ground, no sense of up or down—just the endless, terrifying vastness stretching beyond sight.

"This... this isn't like any other realm," Lena said, her voice trembling. "Where are we?"

"I don't know," I replied, feeling a chill run through me. But I gripped her hand tighter, feeling the spark of determination reignite. "But we have to find out."

****

Author's Note:

Thank you for joining me on this journey *Beyond the Ice Wall*. This story was born from my curiosity about the hidden realms and the untold truths that may lie just beyond our reach. I wanted to explore a world where the boundaries we take for granted—between the known and the unknown, reality and myth—begin to crumble. What would happen if everything we thought we knew about our world turned out to be a carefully crafted illusion?

It has been an adventure to imagine Dr. Cole and Lena's path as they uncover the mind-bending mysteries that lie hidden beyond the ice wall. I hope this story pulled you into the heart of their quest and kept you questioning the nature of reality along the way. If it sparked your imagination or left you wondering about what's truly out there, I'd love to hear your thoughts.

Your reviews mean the world to me and help other readers discover this tale. Please consider sharing your feedback.

More to Come:

The journey doesn't end here. The mysteries revealed in *Beyond the Ice Wall* are just the beginning, and there's much more to discover. Stay tuned for the next chapter, as Dr. Cole and Lena continue to navigate a world where nothing is as it seems. Who knows what doors their next steps will open—or what they'll find waiting on the other side.

Until then, keep asking questions. Sometimes, the truth is closer than we think.

With gratitude,

[Mohamed Elshenawy]

Milton Keynes UK
Ingram Content Group UK Ltd.
UKHW031154251124
451529UK00001B/52

9 798230 875697